BEVERL

ACKNOWLEDGEMENTS:

For BRIAN AND JESSE, with special thanks to Brett Garwood, at Aaron Spelling Productions; and Elizabeth, Josh and all the other young women and men from the Beverly Hills and Hollywood areas who were so enthusiastic and generous with their comments and ideas.

BEVERLY HILLS, 90210

THE FRENCH RIVAL

BY

LAWRENCE CROWN

BOXTREE

First published in the UK 1991
by BOXTREE LIMITED, 36 Tavistock Street,
London WC2E 7PB

1 3 5 7 9 10 8 6 4 2

Cover photograph: E. J. Camp
Photo courtesy: Fox Broadcasting Company

Cover design: Titan Studio

1–85283–671–7

Typeset by Cambrian Typesetters, Frimley, Surrey
Printed and bound in Great Britain by Cox & Wyman Ltd., Reading, Berkshire

A catalogue record of this book is available from the British Library

Chapter One

'When the going gets tough, the tough go surfing.'

'Dylan? What? . . .'

'Sorry, Bren, I just remembered something. I gotta take off.'

Darkly handsome Dylan McKay turned on his heels and broke into a run across the Walsh's manicured front lawn. Golden sunlight glinted off his single earring.

'But, Dylan!' Brenda shouted after him. 'But, Dylan, what about our date? . . .'

He hopped into the driver's seat of his beetle-backed, vintage black Porsche, idling curbside. 'I'll call you.'

Dylan kicked it into gear, slammed down on the gas and, with a smoky squeal of tires, was gone.

One moment it had been a bright Spring day in Beverly Hills, with roses, bougainvillea and magnolias all in colourful bloom. The warm Santa Anna winds blowing off the Southern California deserts were caressing Brenda Walsh's bare arms and legs as she stood on the front steps in her denim shorts and silk blouse, the day's mail – her mother's new Cosmo, some bills and the latest edition of the West Beverly newspaper – cradled loosely in her arms.

Moments earlier she had been smiling at her boyfriend striding up the lawn towards her, and Dylan had been grinning back.

Then a few feet away, he'd stopped. Dylan stared in her direction, as if he'd never seen her before, as if he'd just seen a ghost. Then he took off.

'Dylan, where you going?'

'Sorry, babe, I gotta run.'

'*Where?* Where are you going?'

'I, uh, I'm . . . going surfing. Yeah, I gotta go surf right now . . .'

And suddenly, it wasn't Springtime anymore. Brenda shivered as if she were back in the Minnesota cold, and hugged herself tightly, crumpling the newspaper against her chest. She still hadn't looked at the headline, but Dylan had.

Movie Deal For West Beverly Ex-student it read. *The Parisian Girl Is Back.*

*

'Honey, what's the matter with your sister?'

'Mm-fpn.' Brandon shrugged, waving a piece of toast in the air for emphasis.

Cindy Walsh sighed, turned away from polishing the silver at the kitchen sink and eyed her son with exasperation. 'Don't talk with your mouth full, dear. Chew and swallow.'

Brandon brushed a strand of hair out of his eyes with his free hand and ostentatiously chewed and swallowed. He set the half-eaten toast down on the kitchen table, took a big gulp of milk and wiped his mouth with the back of his hand. He gave his mother a crooked grin.

'I didn't know there was anything the matter with Bren.'

'She's been moping up in her room all morning.'

'No kidding? I had no idea.'

'Well, how could you, Brandon? You've practically slept half the day away.'

'C'mon. Mom, it's Saturday. Besides, Andrea and I were, um, studying last night, uh, until really late.'

Brandon's mother just shook her head. It wasn't that she didn't believe her son exactly. And it wasn't that she didn't like Andrea Zuckerman, the editor of West Beverly High's school paper; actually, she thought that studious, purposeful and ambitious Andrea was a good influence on her sometimes *too* easy-going son. And it wasn't even that she didn't like Dylan McKay, despite his alienated tough-guy pose; it was obvious from how ardently he gazed at Brenda, when he thought no one was looking, that he loved her very much.

It was just that ever since the Spring dance a few weeks before, her two innocent babies had been frolicking around like frisky puppies in the glow of first love. It was all a little *too* frisky for her, and she wished that Jim wasn't gone so much on his seemingly never-ending business trips.

But what was a mother to do, especially one who herself had come of age in the Sixties? It was the Nineties now and this *was* Beverly Hills, mecca for the ultra-rich and the ultra-permissive. There was nothing to do, she reassured herself for the umpteenth time, but to be supportive and understanding and to trust that her children's solid midwestern upbringing in the Minnesota heartland would stand them in good stead here, amidst the many glamorous temptations of the laid-back lifestyle of Southern California.

'I'll talk to her if you want,' Brandon said, adding

insouciantly, 'if you're sure it's not just one of those that-time-of-the-month things.'

'Brandon, *really!*'

'Okay, okay, just a little joke there, Mom.' Brandon stood up and stretched, but stopped abruptly in mid yawn. 'Hey, wait a minute. Weren't Bren and Dylan supposed to go out this morning? Breakfast on Melrose, then some kinda tech fair at the Convention Centre downtown? . . . Uh-oh, trouble in paradise.'

*

Although Brandon often joked about being the big brother, born thirty seconds before his twin sister, he did take his responsibilities as a brother seriously. But when he stuck his head in her room, Brenda was sitting cross-legged on the bed, talking on the telephone, on a party line to Kelly and Donna, her two best girlfriends. She shot Brandon a disgusted, you-men-are-all-alike look and waved him away. He knew her well enough to go.

By then, Brenda understood the problem and she knew that it was bad. Dylan *had* seen a ghost, right there on the front page of the newspaper, and she was a very pretty ghost indeed.

'And famous,' said Donna into the phone. She was sitting by the pool under a jacaranda tree in delicate violet bloom. She picked at the grapefruit half on the table in front of her and gulped down a glistening pink segment. 'All over the world,' she added in her usual tone of maddenly unperturbable normality.

'Plus, Dylan *already* chased after her once,' pert Kelly chimed in from her bedroom, where she was still snuggled under satin sheets in her oversized men's silk pyjamas. 'All the way to Paris.'

'Gee, thanks guys, this is making me feel a whole lot better.'

Donna bit into another wedge of grapefruit. 'Well, Bren,' she remarked levelly. 'You've just got to face facts, haven't you?'

Brenda sighed. 'I wish . . .' Her voice trailed off.

In her luxurious bedroom Kelly sat bolt upright. 'Now, Brenda Walsh, don't you start feeling sorry for yourself! We all know that Dylan McKay is a guy, and guys are *totally* unreliable . . . except when it comes to girls who've dumped them. Then you can always rely on them to chase after what they think they can't have.'

That was a subject where Kelly had plenty of expertise. Ever since she'd dropped *her* long-time boyfriend, convinced that a paragon of perfection like herself could certainly do better, blond Steve Sanders had been in constant dogged pursuit of her. He just seemed completely unable to grasp in his rarely-challenged rich kid's brain that she might genuinely not want to be his steady girlfriend anymore.

'So,' Donna added, 'you just better hope that Nicole's not interested in *him* anymore, now that she's so famous and all.'

'I suppose so,' Brenda replied morosely. 'It's just that I was hoping you guys would come up with something, well, you know, a little constructive.'

'I think that "prepare yourself for the worst" is pretty constructive in this case,' Donna pointed out. 'After all, we're not just talking about *any* little French girl, we're talking about the girl on the cover of the *Sports Illustrated* swimsuit issue.'

'Yeah,' Donna agreed. 'Get ready to forgive and forget . . . *if* he gives you the opportunity. You can't compete with Nicole Didier.'

'None of us can,' Kelly said quietly.

And that's when Brenda realized just how hopeless her situation was: if Kelly Taylor, West Beverly's most perfect blonde and accomplished flirt, said *she* couldn't compete with this Parisian model, then how could Brenda stand a chance?

What a fool she'd been to fall for Dylan McKay! Woefully, Brenda recalled what she'd told her brother months ago, during their first week at the school. Brandon had said he'd made a new friend at West Beverly.

'Who?' she'd asked.

'Dylan McKay,' he'd replied.

'Wake up, Brandon. *Everybody* knows about Dylan McKay,' she'd told him. 'He's, like, major trouble. I heard he got this girl in Paris pregnant.'

Only she'd forgotten her own advice, and she was the one who fell under Dylan's spell. And now she was going to pay the price.

CHAPTER TWO

Dylan McKay sat at the very edge of a granite cliff overlooking a secluded sandy beach north of Malibu and brooded on the past, while the molten sun, touching the far horizon, sent its light dancing across the white-capped waves.

Nicole Didier wasn't an easy girl to forget. After all, you never forget your first love.

Like Brenda, she'd been a transfer student, only she'd come all the way from Paris with her father, the French Consul in Los Angeles. She'd lived in the Ambassador's official residence, an estate in posh Holmby Hills.

Like Brenda, she was a coltish, self-assured girl with short auburn hair and big dark eyes set in a pert gamine's lightly freckled face. She spoke English with a lilting French accent.

They'd met at an outdoor embassy reception, where white-gloved waiters served chilled prawn cocktail and chefs prepared cooked-to-order omelettes and crêpes. At first, Dylan's father, 'Black' Jack McKay, a wheeler-dealer with a reputation for ruthlessness, pushed the two kids at each other. After all, he was manoeuvring for French government financial backing for his latest business scheme.

But who knew the 'kids' would fall in love? Hard, in that way that adults often don't understand.

When Consul Didier found out, he disapproved, and when he was recalled for consultations, he pulled young Nicole out of West Beverly High. She was to return to France and enter a convent school.

'But, *mon père*, I like to stay here with my new schoolmates.'

'*Impossibilité*,' he'd fumed.

Dylan still remembered the stricken look on her tear-stained face when she told him:

'Father says I must go home, *mon cher*.'

'No.'

'*Oui*. I must not disobey.'

'Then I'll follow you.'

And that's exactly what he'd done, cashing in the stocks and bonds accumulated from previous birthdays and flying overnight to Paris at the beginning of the Spring break.

He'd stayed in a little hotel near Montparnasse for one storybook week. A famous French fashion photographer, spotting Nicole sitting and holding hands with him in an outdoor café, took one look at Nicole's glowing face and immediately arranged a photo shoot. It was Nicole Didier's first step on the road to becoming one of the world's biggest new fashion sensations. For a time, it seemed that everything was going to turn out alright.

But Dylan hadn't counted on running into his father, an avid tennis buff, one day at the French Open.

'What the hell are you doing *here*, boy?' he'd thundered. Then he saw wide-eyed Nicole peeking out fearfully from behind his son. 'Her? *Her?* Are you trying to sabotage me?'

'But, Dad—'

'Don't you know that her father thinks you're corrupting his innocent little girl?'

'*Tout au contraire, Monsieur Mee-Kay*, it is not at all like that. Dylan and I are so—'

'It's not *your* opinion I'm concerned about, Missy.'

'You can't talk to Nicole like that!'

In the end, it was a fight which shocked even the jaded French – shouts and shoves and smashed cocktail glasses, and finally *gendarmes* to escort Dylan to the plane which was to fly him back to the States.

From then, he'd been estranged from his father. And he hadn't seen Nicole since.

*

Now, she seemed everywhere – billboards, magazine covers, commercials on TV for Parisian Girl Perfume – except out here on this lonely point overlooking the deserted beach north of Malibu.

The first pearly light of dawn cast Dylan's shadow across the breakers below. He'd been brooding alone all night. Wearily, he stood up and trudged back to his Porsche parked on the sandy bluff behind him.

Forty minutes later, he was cruising down Sunset, the busy boulevard nearly deserted in the early Sunday morning hours. There she was again. In Cinemascope-sized profile, Nicole's face stared back on the giant billboard across from Spago.

Parisian Girl Perfume, the legend on the billboard read. *The Scent of Springtime.*

A few blocks East, he pulled into the driveway of Le Bel Age hotel. In the lobby he stopped at the desk to check for messages: one from Steve Sanders, two from Brandon and *four* from Brenda, the last at 2.20 a.m.

In the corporate suite where he stayed, Dylan kicked off his shoes and flopped face down on the bed. He was bone-tired. *I'll just close my eyes for a few minutes*, he thought, *then I'll call Bren.*

But tension and exhaustion had taken their toll, and Dylan McKay slept right around the clock. And when he finally awakened, it was Monday morning and he had to rush to shower, shave and change in time to make school.

And by then it was too late for explanations. Brenda had been left in the dark with her own fears and frustrations for two whole days with no word from her boyfriend, and she was coldly furious.

CHAPTER THREE

'I think this is just disgusting!' Andrea Zuckerman declared, as she and Brandon walked up the broad steps leading to West Beverly High's front entrance. Her sweeping gesture took in the knots of excited students on the school's front lawn and the TV news vans crowding along the sidewalk, their masts raised and pointed at the relay station on Mount Wilson. 'I mean, even *Entertainment Tonight* is here.'

And in fact, just outside the big front doors, an *E.T.* field producer was interviewing Kelly, in designer jeans and a copper-and-black leotard top, and Donna, who was wearing an oversize black jumpsuit decorated with a plethora of zippers. Andrea and Brandon stopped just out of camera range to listen.

'Oh, yes,' Kelly enthused with a shake of her blonde locks. 'Nicole and I were really, *really* good friends when she was here.'

'We knew she was going to go on to great things even back then,' Donna added with utmost seriousness.

'God,' Andrea whispered into Brandon's ear. 'The

blonde bopsie twins! Look at how they're preening for the cameras. I think I'll write an editorial about corrupting academic values for a little cheap show-business publicity.'

'Well, that would work okay,' Brandon said, holding open the door for Andrea, who was both his new girlfriend and the editor of the school paper. 'But that would still be one person's opinion.'

'Meaning?'

'Meaning you could either talk about it or you could show it . . . Assign somebody to cover this paragon of beauty and success on a typical day in L.A. *Show* our readers the shallowness of fame.'

Andrea stopped and eyed him suspiciously. 'Brandon Walsh. What are you suggesting? I suppose *you* want the assignment?'

'*Me?*' Brandon looked genuinely surprised. 'Now that you mention it, I do think a male reporter would be better for this story. Then nobody could accuse the reporter of cattiness or jealousy . . . But I can understand how you wouldn't want me to do it. After all, if this Nicole is as hot as everybody says . . .'

Andrea pursed her lips. 'You don't think I'm secure enough to assign *you*, is that it?' Brandon grinned and shrugged. 'Well, buster, you're dead wrong. The story's a good idea, and you're the one who thought of it, so it's your piece.'

Andrea spun on her heel and started away. 'Deadline's Wednesday, five o'clock sharp!'

Brandon gave her a mock salute. 'Aye-aye, chief.' As he strolled towards Tech class, he felt quite satisfied with himself. *Who says I don't understand female psychology?* he thought smugly.

*

Brandon found Dylan hunched over his usual green-glowing computer terminal, in a far corner of the dimly lighted Tech class. He slid into the seat at the adjoining console.

Dylan glanced up. 'Yo, Brandon, what's happening?'

'*You're* happening, dude.' They dapped, a variation of the complicated, palm-slapping handshake that had started out in the ghetto and now was the universal greeting among hip young males everywhere.

'I hope your sister still thinks so.'

'Hmmm.' Brandon stroked his chin. 'Well, now that you mention it, man, I haven't seen her this steamed since we were both nine-years-old and I cooked her favourite Barbie in the microwave.'

'I guess I can't blame her.'

'Something about you skipping out on a date, not calling all weekend, that sort of thing.' He gave his pal a sympathetic look. '*Girls*. Who can figure 'em?'

'Yeah, well, I know. But I'm gonna apologize to her. It's just, I had a lot of thinking to do.'

Brandon eyed his friend. 'You're looking a little wasted, man. You're not drinking again, are you? I mean, if you are, it's okay. I'm here for you, y'know, just like you were for me. We can both go back to A.A.'

'Nah, it's nothing like that.' Dylan turned back to the computer screen. He stared into it as if trying to see the future.

'If you don't want to talk about it, that's okay too,' Brandon said. 'I'll back off.'

Dylan sighed heavily. 'No, I'll tell you. You're gonna hear about it anyway.'

'Go for it,' Brandon said softly.

'You remember back when I started to get together with your sister?'

'How could I forget?' Brandon replied dryly. Their father had been vehemently opposed when Dylan and Brenda had first started dating, citing Jack McKay's black reputation in business circles and noting that 'the seed doesn't fall far from the tree'. At first, Brandon, too, had doubted Dylan's intentions. Finally, he'd talked to Dylan about it.

'You remember that night you were being the big brother, protecting your little sister?'

Brandon, still a little embarrassed, grimaced at the memory. 'Yeah, I remember I was really on my high horse and gave you lots of attitude. I wanted to know – no, I *demanded* to know – if your intentions toward my sister were honourable, or if this was just another meaningless conquest for the great Dylan McKay?'

Dylan leaned in toward him, so that the green glow from the computer console washed over his face. 'And you remember what I told you? You remember what I said?'

'Sure . . . I guess so. Let's see: You said you cared a lot for Brenda.'

'Yeah, what else?'

Brandon chuckled mirthlessly. 'You said it was none of my damn business.'

'Yeah.' Dylan rubbed his chin reflectively. 'I guess I did do that. I'd forgotten about that part. I guess you weren't the only one with attitude that night. You remember what else?'

Brandon thought a moment, staring up at the ceiling then back down at the computer screen, blank as his memory. 'I dunno . . . Wait a minute.' He snapped his fingers. 'I got it! You said the only time you ever felt that way before was when you went nuts over some little transfer student, some Parisian girl—

'*Holy cow!* . . .'

Every head in Tech jerked up in their direction. Brandon lowered his voice to a whisper. 'I'll be damned! Nicole Didier, the one on the cover of the swimsuit issue? *She's* your Parisian girl!'

Chapter Four

First impressions, Brandon wrote in his reporter's spiral notebook, *are of a pep rally or maybe a rock concert – not a lunch-hour school assembly.*

The auditorium is jammed. The first time I've seen that at a voluntary assembly. The blue-and-white bunting is up on the walls and draped from the stage, where the cheerleaders are doing their routines, getting the kids psyched – as if they needed it.

The Parisian girl's vast entourage is milling around up front – beefy security guards, a hair dresser, a make-up lady, a photographer wearing a checkered kerchief around his neck, a middle-aged, dour-faced lady in a starched uniform, who could be a tutor or maybe a nanny. And, of course, Max.

Max is a beefy little bald guy who looks like he slept in his seersucker suit. There's an unlit cigar jammed in his big mouth. He is Miss Parisian Girl's personal press agent.

Ol' Max is red with apoplexy, arguing with Mr Strickland about the propriety of giving out free perfume samples to the assembly and letting the TV cameras in (the Vice Principal gives in on the perfume, but keeps the cameras out).

Steve Sanders, doing his Big Man on Campus routine, is buttonholing Max – something about how his mother, Samantha, is a big TV star and wants to meet Nicole Didier and perhaps have her do a guest spot on the show. But give Max credit, he knows a con job when he hears one, and when Steve says he wants a private audience with Miss Parisian Girl, Max shines him on.

That's when I come over, introduce myself as an enquiring mind writing for the student paper, on assignment to follow his client around through a typical day. He's tempted to give me the brush-off, too, but then he has second thoughts. 'Could be good P.R., kid,' he says. 'Come see me after the assembly. I'll run it by Miss Didier.'

By now, the whole place stinks of Parisian Girl Perfume, and everybody's going nuts, as if both Michael Jackson and Madonna were about to come out on stage. Everybody, that is, except my sister, sitting dead centre between Donna and Kelly, with her arms folded tightly in front of her chest. And Andrea, of course, who isn't even here.

Mr Strickland finally mounts the stage. When he finally gets the crowd calmed down, he delivers nothing but a string of platitudes – about Making Good, about Truth and Beauty, about Multi-Cultural Education and so forth.

Then he gets to the part about an honorary West Beverly High degree for the accomplished Miss P.G. Perfume, who has always had such strong ties to the school (there are a few snickers here; Brenda looks stricken and I look around for Dylan, but he's a no-show, too). And then, finally, Mr S. gets to the point, and the point, naturally, is money – the money the perfume company is putting up for the Nicole Didier Scholarship Fund, to promote U.S.–French cultural programmes and support foreign students at West Beverly.

Then the lights go down and we have a little audio-visual interlude:

Rapid-fire video stills flash by on a screen that descends from the ceiling at the back of the stage – Baby Nicole with her proud Daddy . . . Pre-teen Nicole posing precociously in front of the Eiffel Tower (a portent of supermodeldom-to-come) . . . Nicole in a J.V. cheerleader uniform and pom-poms, leaping in the gym (was that Dylan in the background of the photo?) . . . Nicole as poised young hostess at one of her father's French Embassy soirées . . .

Then we switch to big-screen video, disco music kicks in, and we have another montage, this time Nicole – the Modelling Years:

Nicole posing prettily, twirling and parading down haute-couture catwalks and in studios, under bright lights, in front of whirring fans and smoke machines, wearing a succession of demure little frocks and elegant evening gowns . . .

Then the obligatory beach shots: a lithe, sexy Nicole frolicking in the waves, wearing the skimpiest of bikinis . . . and at this the auditorium (or at least its male contingent) erupts in a cacophony of wolf whistles and rabid dog barks, with Steve's baritone woof-woof and the high-pitched nerdy howls of David and Scott, the two inseparable freshmen, rising above the rest . . .

Finally, the lights come up and there she is, standing alone at the centre of the stage.

Got to admit: she looks great. That short reddish-brown hair, the snub nose, the spray of freckles, the huge eyes. She's wearing a demure little polka-dot sundress.

Nicole says a few words in lightly accented English, something about feeling honoured and happy to be back at West Beverly, of which she has so many fond memories. And then she's gone.

*

Feeling sheepish, Brandon followed the crush of wannabes and hangers-on out of the auditorium and outside on to the lawn. At the centre of it all was the demure French model, who was quickly ushered to a camera position near her entourage's stretch limos, where she posed for the paparazzi and patiently endured how-do-you-feel questions from the rabid TV press.

Up close, Brandon noticed, she was every bit as pretty as on the big screen. Suddenly, fast-talking Max was at his elbow.

'This is your lucky day, kid. You can imagine how many interview requests Miss Didier has – *The Times*, *People*, *E.T.* – but we talked it over and she's gonna give you a shot!'

The press agent held out his pudgy hands as if framing a headline. 'Picture this, kid: "A Day in the Life of Hollywood's Most Sought-After Young Lady",' he enthused. 'How about it, huh? Great stuff! Now ya gotta be ready to roll early, I'm talkin' dawn here, and go on 'till late. She's a real little French dynamo an' we got every expensive minute booked. Know what I mean?'

'But the thing is, she's givin' you this shot, and *only* you, 'cause she's got a soft spot for this school of yours.'

Brandon was tempted to reply that it was all because the P.R. man had probably figured he could stage-manage the news better if he was dealing with a student journalist.

But just then, out of the corner of his eye, he saw Dylan approaching, his long black coat flapping, eyes hidden behind shades.

Nicole Didier saw him too and, to Max's horror, she stopped in mid-soundbite and rushed towards him. The assembled TV cameras tracked after her.

'Dee-lan! Dee-lan, bay-bee!'

The cameras were rolling and the paparazzi were snapping away as she jumped happily into his arms, wrapping her hands around his neck. Brandon was astonished, but it was nothing to what happened next.

She took Dylan by the hand and tugged him in the direction of the long black limousine. He seemed to resist at first, but she pulled the reluctant Dylan along. When they reached the limo's open rear door, Nicole leaned in and took a bundle from the woman in the starched uniform.

Nicole turned and held it out for Dylan to see. As the paparazzi went wild, Dylan gingerly took the bundle from her.

It was a sight which made Brandon draw in his breath sharply. Dylan McKay held a baby in his arms.

Chapter Five

'Oh, my god!' Kelly was in her bedroom, chattering on the phone with Donna. Her television was on, with the sound down. 'Quick, turn on Channel Five.'

On the other end of the line, Donna gasped. The scene on the news was Nicole and Dylan . . . and the baby. 'I'm calling Brenda.'

'So am I.'

But they both got an engaged tone. Brandon had taken the phone off the hook. He glanced over at his mother, who was staring at the same picture being repeated on TV screens all over Beverly Hills.

'Poor Brenda,' Cindy Walsh said softly. Involuntarily, she looked over her shoulder, towards the stairs leading up to their bedrooms. Ever since the end of the school day, Brenda had been closeted in her room. She hadn't even come down for dinner.

*

In the cocktail lounge of the Hilton hotel overlooking

the Chicago riverfront Jim Walsh was having the last business meeting of a long and busy day. His client was rattling on about fixed costs and built-in escalators and other contractual arcana, but Jim wasn't listening. With his drink forgotten halfway to his lips, he sat transfixed by the nationally syndicated tabloid TV show on the bar-room screen.

'Jim? . . . Say, *Jim!*'

'Huh?' Brenda and Brandon's father pulled his gaze away from the television set. 'Oh, sorry, Fred. It's just that I thought I recognized the kid on TV.'

Fred laughed heartily. 'On *that* sleazy show? I seriously doubt you'd ever know the likes of the people that get on a show like that.'

Jim chuckled without conviction. 'Of course I wouldn't, Fred. Now let's see, where were we?'

'Just finalising the last few details on a five-million-dollar deal,' Fred said with entrepreneurial gusto.

'So we were.' Abruptly, Jim Walsh stood up, clapping Fred on the back. 'Hold that thought a minute, pal. I've gotta go make a phone call.'

But when he tried to call home, he found the line busy too.

*

Andrea Zuckerman replaced the telephone in its cradle and carefully put her glasses back on. She stared at the unopened stack of books in front of her. She was beginning to have second thoughts about the assignment she had given Brandon.

It wasn't as if she was worried about him; Brandon was much too sensible a boy to get swept up in the Nico-mania that had gripped the rest of the school, she told herself. It was just that this embarrassing Dylan business might tilt him too far in the other direction; after all, how could he help not feeling *some* hostility towards the Parisian model, considering her involvement with his best friend and the effect that must be having on his sister?

She just wished the Walsh's phone hadn't been busy for the past half-hour. Again, Andrea looked at the unopened books. Best to forget it, she told herself, there was tomorrow's Biology class to study for and, besides, she could always talk it over with Brandon then.

But if she'd known that Brandon wouldn't be in school, that he'd take the day off to go 'on assignment', Andrea might've kept dialling all night.

*

Beep . . . Beep . . . Beep . . .

Dylan slammed the phone down in disgust. For a fraction of a second he considered throwing it against the wall, but suddenly it rang.

'Bren? . . .'

There was a deep, salacious chuckle at the other end of the line. 'I don't think so, bud. Somethin' tells me you're not gonna be hearing from *that* babe again.'

'Sanders? What the hell do you want?'

'Chill out, McKay,' Steve Sanders said into the telephone, preening in front of his bedroom mirror as he talked. 'You're not getting an attitude, are you, now that you're the Love God with the Love Child I've been watching on TV?'

'Gimme a break, Steve.'

'So how about putting in a good word with your French honey? My mom wants to meet her.'

'I don't know Steve. It's not the way you think—'

'Sure, sure, man. You just do what you can, okay?'

'Okay, Steve,' Dylan said with an exasperated sigh. Agreeing was easier than arguing or trying to explain.

'Now you're talkin', man . . . Oh yeah, one other thing. Considering what's gone down and everything, you wouldn't mind if I asked Brenda out, would ya?'

Click. The line went dead. 'What the hell?' Steve Sanders exclaimed. He began to redial, but back at Le Bel Age, Dylan was already striding out to his car.

*

Even though the Walshes lived only two blocks north of bustling Sunset, on Hillcrest, the Beverly Hills night was country-quiet. Outside her bedroom window, Brenda could hear the loud chirping of crickets.

She sat on her bed in the dark, still wearing her lace-edged white shorts that were covered by the oversize gold-and-black checked shirt she'd long ago appropriated from her father. On her feet, stretched out in front of her, were white gym socks. She leaned back against the headboard and thought about the confusion in her life: It had certainly been more comfortable and predictable back in Minnesota.

Beverly Hills was awash in big money, glamour and big temptations. Why had she ever given in to Dylan McKay? How could she have been so wrong about him? Sure, he was smart, strong, sensitive and independent. But he was also a recovering alcoholic, moody and (where his father was concerned at least) subject to sullenness and rage. She had been so sure about him . . .

The familiar deep-throated purr of a Porsche engine downshifting startled her out of her reverie.

There was no sense in waking the house, so she tiptoed downstairs and slipped out on to the front steps, just in time to see Dylan – still in his trademark long black coat and shades, looking every inch the outlaw – hop out of the car. He approached her warily.

'You're not gonna hit me or anything?' he asked with mock (or was it mocking? she wondered) concern.

'I ought to.' Brenda glared, stony-faced, at Dylan. 'What's gotten into you, Dylan? . . . Isn't this all a little melodramatic, I mean, for a guy with your cool, your style?'

Very deliberately, Dylan took off his dark glasses. 'Yeah, I guess I see what you mean,' he said ruefully, shifting his weight to one leg. 'Look, Bren, all this media-hype crap, I just hope you know that's just something that . . . happened. I mean, I happened to walk into it all, know what I mean?

'Anyway, in about fifteen minutes, all the media hype will go someplace else and people will just forget about this.'

'Sure, just as soon as they throw away their copy of this week's *National Enquirer*.'

Dylan smiled at her caustic little joke. It was an affectionate smile, Brenda thought, noticing the familiar warm twinkle in his eyes. It almost reassured her.

'Anyway,' she continued, returning the look with a tentative smile of her own. 'You know darn well that's not the part that upsets me. I don't care what *people* think; I care what you think, and how it makes *me* feel. And I want to know just what's going on.'

'That's the problem, Bren.' Dylan gazed directly into her eyes. 'I *don't know* what I think. I don't know what I *should* think . . . or do.' He glanced over his shoulder, back into the night, then looked back at her. 'I know what the kids at school have been saying, "Dylan got this girl pregnant in Paris" and all, but I swear to you, Bren, *I* never knew for sure. Those stories only started after Nick—'

(*Nick?* Brenda thought to herself.)

'—got famous and started getting into the gossip columns and they started saying this stuff about her being the hot, new, young *unmarried* French teen model with a kid, who travelled everywhere with her own nanny.

'Today was the very first time I have ever even seen the kid. I still don't really know if it's true.'

'Really?' She arched an eyebrow skeptically. 'But what about you and Miss Teen Model, you and, ah, "Nick"?'

'That's the thing, Bren, I'm not at all sure it *is* about me and Nicole . . . Or even about me and you.

'You know, when the cameras stopped rolling and those vultures finally flew away, we talked . . . oh, for maybe thirty seconds, until her "handlers" whisked her away . . . and she seemed, well, different . . . Harder, maybe.'

'So *what* is it all about, Dylan?' Brenda asked softly.

Dylan's brow furrowed. 'The kid,' he said solemnly.

'If that's really my child out there, what do I do? What's my responsibility?' He brushed her cheek lightly with the back of his hand. 'I've learned a lot about responsibility from you Walshes . . . So *now* what do I do? I never meant for this to happen, but if it has, I've got to figure out what to do?'

After a moment, Brenda said, 'I understand.' It was a hard thing to say, but then she said something harder still.

'I think you need to have a serious talk with Nicole. See how you feel about . . . things. Talk about . . . *her* baby.'

Then she said the hardest thing she'd ever had to say. 'Until you sort things out, Dylan, I don't think we should see each other.'

Then she stood on tiptoe, brushed his cheek with her lips, turned and went inside.

*

Brenda stood in the bathroom that separated her bedroom and Brandon's and listened. No radio or TV and no sign of light. Quietly, she pushed open the closed door a crack.

'Brandon?' she whispered into the dark. 'Are you asleep?'

'Mmm, yeah, Bren.' He rolled over under the covers and squinted up at her through sleep-bleared eyes. 'What's up?'

'Dylan and I broke up. At least for a while.'

'Gee, Brenda, I'm really sorry.' He sat up, rubbed his eyes with the back of his fists and yawned. 'Dylan's a dork.'

'It's okay, Brandon, I broke up with him. I don't want to wait around while he decides what to do, or let him have his little fling and then take him back. That's what Kelly and Donna think I should do.'

'They're dorks, too. And you're the best thing that ever happened to Dylan McKay. I'm surprised he doesn't know that.'

'Thank you, Brandon,' Brenda said quietly, grateful for the unswerving support and feeling she'd always had from her brother since they'd been kids.

'You know, Brandon, I don't want you saying anything on my account or pressurising Dylan or anything. You know, I just want him to have his space.'

'Sure, Brenda.'

'And that girl, you're still interviewing her, right?'

'Not if you don't want me to, Bren.'

'No, it's okay. You've got your assignment and you

just go and do it. Be professional, it has nothing to do with all this.'

'Yeah.'

'What I'm trying to say is, don't mention anything about Dylan, about me, you know, *us*, when you interview her. Okay?'

'Yeah, Brenda. Okay.'

'Thanks, Brandon. Goodnight.'

' 'Night, Brenda.'

She tiptoed back out and went to her own room. But she didn't turn out the light.

It was nearly dawn by the time Brenda finally fell into a troubled sleep, and by then Brandon was already in the shower, getting ready for his interview early that day.

CHAPTER SIX

Brandon approached the distinctive pink stucco of the venerable Beverly Hills Hotel with more than just a touch of Midwestern awe. The place, with its private chalets and chic Polo Lounge, had been a magnet for Hollywood celebrities and dealmakers since the prewar Golden Age.

For a moment, Brandon stood in the coolly gleaming lobby, just a kid wearing jeans and an ancient herringbone jacket over a blue cotton sports shirt open at the neck, carrying his green bookbag over one shoulder, adrift in a sea of tailored business suits and highly polished Florsheims. The arrow on a small brass plate indicated the Polo Lounge was off to the right.

Max and Nicole's photographer were already there, seated at a red-leather banquette along one of the palm-green walls, a "power" table, where they could see everyone who came in, and, more importantly, be *seen* by everyone who came in.

The tuxedo'd maitre d' guarding the entranceway

gave Brandon the once-over. 'May I help you, sir?' he inquired in his stentorian, faintly disapproving voice.

'Hey, kid, over here!' Max waved his unlit cigar, saving Brandon from having to stammer out an explanation, and the maitre d' immediately snapped to and led him to their table.

'Have a seat, kid, she'll be right down.' Max pointed the well-chewed cigar at a profusion of croissants and breakfast pastries, fresh juices and steaming coffees laid out over the Polo Lounge's trademark pink tablecloth. 'Eat, eat! Go on, help yourself.'

Brandon slid in next to the photographer, who introduced himself as Roland St. Gilles. He was in his thirties, tall and pale with grey-flecked dark hair, and was dressed in black trousers and a baggy black turtleneck. He spoke in a husky whisper, with a vaguely European accent.

Roland was the photographer who'd first discovered Nicole, 'way back in Gay Paree', said Max expansively, leaning back, lighting up with his gold Dunhill and puffing away, while Brandon, drinking orange juice and biting into a kiwi-and-strawberry cream tart, eyed him curiously.

Max exhaled a thick cloud of blue smoke and said, 'Now Roland's shooting her for this photo book he's doing.'

'Roly likes to shoot young girls,' he added with a smirk.

Roland St. Gilles shrugged with Gallic self-deprecation. He lit a Gitane and nodded in the general direction of the maitre d'. 'She comes now,' he said casually, but his narrowed eyes burned with an intensity that Brandon didn't understand.

Nicole Didier didn't so much walk towards them as strut, the very picture of sexy self-assurance, a young woman who knew her flashing legs and walk had captured the rapt attention of every man.

She was wearing a short, simple, but skintight, lemon-yellow tube dress, tied at her waist by a colourful silk scarf. A single strand of pearls hung from her long neck. Her big eyes were hidden behind even bigger round sunglasses.

'*Bonjour*,' she trilled lightly, sitting next to Max and giving Brandon a coquettish smile. While Nicole poured herself black coffee and lit one of Roland's Gitanes, Max did the introductions.

'But I do not remember you from my time at West Beverly.'

'I'm a transfer student, Miss Didier, from Minnesota. It's my first year here.'

'Ah, zee Twin Cities, zee ten-thousand lakes . . . But do call me Nicole or, if you prefer, Nickie.'

'Alright . . . Nicole.'

'It is very different here, *n'est-ce pas?*'

'Tougher in a lot of ways than back home. But I think adjusting to Beverly Hills must be tougher for a girl. I know it was hard on my sister.'

Don't say it, the warning voice in Brandon's head admonished. *Remember, you promised Brenda*. But he blurted it out anyway.

'I think you know this guy she's been going out with.'

'Yes?'

'Dylan McKay.'

Nicole slipped off her sunglasses and shot Max a sharp disapproving glance. He fidgeted uncomfortably; making sure Miss Didier wasn't surprised was part of his high-paid P.R. job.

Nicole turned back to Brandon, looking at him as if seeing him for the first time. 'So . . . then shall this be the – how do you say? – interview *adverse*?'

Brandon couldn't help smiling. Her directness was very appealing. Despite the entourage of more-or-less cynical and weary adults, he guessed this was one girl who took some care to manage her own life. 'I just thought you should know, I guess so you didn't find out later. You know, truth in journalistic packaging, and all that.

'You should know, too, I don't do hatchet jobs. I go straight down the line, just like they teach you in school. My assignment is to do a day-in-the-life, and that is exactly what I aim to do.'

'*Formidable!* What a declaration!'

'I didn't mean to come off like Mister Crusading Journalist or anything. I just wanted to make sure you knew I was going to treat you just like I would, uh, Christie Brinkley . . . or any other beautiful superstar model.'

Nicole stared at him for a second, then giggled like a schoolgirl. 'What a good joke!' she clapped. 'Please though, Isabelle Rosellini,' she begged with mock gravity.

This time, Brandon laughed. Their smiles met. For just a second, they were like kids at a dinner table, sharing a joke the adults didn't get.

St. Gilles looked exasperated. He checked his Rolex. 'We have to get started soon. Aren't you eating breakfast again, Nicole?'

'You know I'm watching my weight, Roland,' she replied, exhaling a thin stream of smoke.

'Nicole . . .'

'Alright, alright.' She stubbed out the cigarette. 'I'll have my vitamins with an orange juice.' To Brandon, she added, 'Roly thinks he's my poppa.'

The photographer seemed oddly nonplussed. 'Really, Nicole, someone has to watch out for your own good.'

'And somebody's gotta get this show on the road,' Max interjected, pulling a typed itinerary out of his jacket, while Nicole drank a large glass of juice in three big gulps.

Brandon found himself watching her with a peculiar sort of pleasure. He was actually beginning to relax, here with these Beautiful People in this Famous Place.

Not bad for a kid from Minnesota, he thought, giving the fabulous young model a frankly appraising glance.

She smiled back at him, putting the empty glass down on the cloth-covered table. She wiped her perfect red lips with the back of one long, graceful hand. 'Where do we go first, Max?' she asked.

Chapter Seven

Brenda and Andrea were both having one of those days, one of those ultra-trying, downright infuriating school days.

You know the kind: The new Spielberg spectacular opens over the weekend, or there's something new and outrageous from Madonna; and on Monday, everybody at school is talking about it – in the halls, at their lockers, between and during classes . . .

Or, perhaps, a car packed full of kids cruising Sunset on Saturday night who spot the West Beverly Wildcats' star quarterback and a totally perfect cheerleader, with a goody-goody reputation, staggering together out of Gazzara's, where the heavy-metal headbangers hang out, and they're making out, right there in the street. And, on Monday, everybody at school is talking about it.

The only difference this time, Andrea thought irritably, as she made her way down the crowded hallway to Biology class, was that it was already Tuesday and the buzz at school, fuelled no doubt by the tabloids and trash TV, was *still* about Nicole Didier.

And, Andrea was discovering, there were plenty of scandalous stories. *Why* had she ever assigned Brandon, practically her own boyfriend, to spend the day with a girl like that?

'Didya hear?' a gawky freshman named Scott, who, she thought, looked like Dennis the Menace and dressed like a retarded twelve-year-old kid, was saying to his sidekick – geeky, wavy-haired David, as Andrea walked past. 'She's been living on her own since she was *our* age?'

'Yeah, yeah,' David replied, eyeing up every half-way decent-looking girl they passed. 'Her mother died in a plane crash and her dad's some big-deal French diplomat. Nicole went wild on the Euro-trash party circuit for a while. Then her dad got sent to Tokyo or someplace and she got this career thing going, modelling all over, always travelling with all those people, that what-you-call-it.'

Andrea found it all so, so . . . juvenile. Still, she couldn't resist correcting David as she passed. ' "Entourage", that's the word you're looking for. And it's not Tokyo, it's Beijing.'

'Huh?' The two freshmen stopped and blinked uncomprehendingly at her.

'I said, *Monsieur* Didier is the French ambassador to China, *not* Japan, and he lives in Beijing, not Tokyo. Where do you get your information, the *Enquirer* or the *Sun*?'

As she stalked off, Scott squeaked, 'Jeez, what's the matter with her?'

'I dunno.' David was genuinely puzzled. 'What's the matter with the *Sun* anyway?'

*

When Brenda got to her locker, Donna and Kelly were already there. Kelly was wearing a rust linen jumpsuit and Donna a blue silk dress, but, as Brenda saw the expressions on their faces, she thought ruefully they might as well both be wearing black.

'Will you guys cut it out!'

'What?'

'You're both looking at me like someone just died. So just cut it out. Okay?'

They both gave her their best phony smiles, and Brenda laughed despite herself.

Kelly grabbed her by the elbow. 'Okay, now you've got that out of your system, tell us what happened? Did you dump Dylan? What did he say?'

'What did *you* say?' Donna chorused.

Brenda hung her oversized denim jacket on a peg in the locker and smoothed the front of her navy jumper. 'Alright, alright. But you can't tell anybody. Swear?'

'. . . Hope to die,' Donna mumbled, making a vague gesture in the air.

Kelly held up two fingers. 'Scout's honour,' she intoned.

Donna elbowed her in the ribs. 'You were never a scout.'

'Doesn't matter. It's the principle of the thing that counts.' She batted her big button eyes. 'Go on, Brenda. Unburden yourself. We're your friends.'

'Well . . . okay. He came over last night. Late. We talked.' Brenda frowned thoughtfully. 'I think it's the idea of the baby that's messing him up . . .

'Anyway, I told Dylan we shouldn't see each other for a while and that he should talk things over with Nicole.'

'You *what*?' Kelly couldn't believe her ears. 'That's practically throwing him at her!'

'That's *exactly* throwing him at her,' Donna observed. 'Are you crazy, Brenda?'

'I'd be crazy if I didn't stand up for myself,' Brenda declared. 'And if I was right to be with him in the first place, then what do I have to worry about now?'

And, with a toss of her hair and an air of jaunty confidence she didn't remotely feel, Brenda Walsh marched off to class.

*

Dylan couldn't keep his mind on school. Not when Nicole and her child – *their* child? – was out there, and there was important business to settle . . . the kind of business that would affect the rest of his life.

But how to find her? He didn't even know which hotel she was staying at.

'Hey, bud.'

Dylan looked up. It was Steve Sanders, and Dylan wasn't in the mood for his breezy chat.

'How about that Brandon, man? Of all the dumb luck.'

'Steve.' Dylan held up a restraining finger. There was something fatuous about Sanders' all-American, blonde-and-blue-eyed good looks and a smugness about himself that Dylan found irritating, despite the fact that he, Brandon and Steve often hung out after school together. 'Steve, what the hell are you talking about?'

'I was just in Miss Watson's office. She was telling her T.A. that Brandon Walsh wouldn't be in class today because he had a school paper assignment to spend the day with Nicole Didier, your French babe.'

'Damn.' Dylan slammed his fist down on the desktop. 'Damn, damn, damn!' If only he'd talked to Brandon, he'd know how to find her.

'Tough, huh, man? Your best buddy *and* your chick.'

'She's not my "chick", and it's not that anyway, Steve. It's just that Brandon could've told me how to get hold of her. I don't know where she's staying.'

'*You* don't know where she's staying? Wow, man! I thought for sure you and she would be at her place, doing the do.'

'You're a fine human being, Steven,' Dylan said sarcastically. 'A real credit to the gender, know what I mean?'

'Lighten up, McKay.' Steve adjusted his shirt collar. 'When did you start sensitivity training?'

But Dylan wasn't listening. 'Wait a minute. Your mother's in that TV show, right?'

'Yeah, *Hartley House*. So?'

'So, don't all the celebrities know how to get a hold of each other? Call each other's agents, stuff like that?'

'Probably.' Clearly, Steve Sanders didn't have a clue, but that didn't keep him from trying to project a bluff certainty. 'So?'

'So, what if you called your mother and had her find out where Nicole's staying? It would be easy.'

'I don't know, she's a pretty busy lady.'

Dylan thought a moment. 'You'd like to go out with Nicole, wouldn't you? It'd be a big deal, right, a real coup, an evening on the town with this famous model?'

Steve's fevered mind immediately kicked into party-down gear. 'It'd be awesome, man. If half the things the tabloids say about her are true . . .'

'Oh, Nick was always one for a good time. Clubbing 'till dawn. Crystal and caviar . . .'

'You'd fix me up? You'd do *that* for me? With *her*?'

'I'd introduce you,' Dylan said carefully. 'What happens after that is up to you. But, hey, you've got all the moves, dude. All you need is to get next to her, right?'

'Yeah.' Steve thought about the possibilities for a moment. 'Okay, I'll do it.'

And as it turned out, Samantha Sanders' agent subscribed to something called Celebrity Service, which faxed him, each business day, a list of all the out-of-town celebrities currently in Los Angeles and the hotels at which they were staying.

Chapter Eight

West Beverly High was practically in the shadow of Century City, but Brandon didn't get there much. Not like Brenda, whose best girlfriends, Donna and Kelly, practically lived at Bullocks and the other stores in the vast shopping centre there.

For Brandon, Century City was still merely the twin glass-and-steel towers he used to see back in Minnesota, when he was watching the opening credits of *L.A. Law* on TV.

'Yeah, kid, once all this used to be the Fox studio's backlot,' Max was saying. Through the limo's tinted windows, Brandon took in the vista of luxury hotels, high-rise office buildings and elegant restaurants and theatres. 'Yeah, I used to be unit publicist on all those B-movie Westerns they used to make here back in the Fifties. Of course, Marilyn was around then.'

'Really,' Brandon said politely. 'Marilyn Monroe?'

'Oh yeah, she was just a starlet, but everybody knew she was going to be a really big star. Then the studio made *Cleopatra*, but that was way back before you kids were born, and TV was coming in, so they sold off the real estate and built all this.'

'What happened to the studio?' Brandon wanted to know. He was sitting in the limo's jump seat, facing Nicole, who was between Max and Roland. 'Oh, it's still there,' Max said. 'Down on Pico. In fact, you can see the *Hello, Dolly* street sets from the penthouse in the Century Plaza Hotel.'

Roland was fiddling with his cameras, while Nicole listened politely and nonchalantly filled a crystal flute with bubbly champagne. As she lit another cigarette, her fourth of the morning, Brandon glanced down at his watch. It was only 9 a.m.

*

'Looks like the start of the L.A. Marathon,' Brandon said, gazing out at the hundreds of shoppers, most of them women – shop-till-you-drop Beverly Hills matrons and hooky-playing schoolgirls alike – crowding the aisles around the Bullocks' perfume department.

He was standing with Max, who had been happily puffing on his cigar in violation of the posh store's no-smoking signs until chastized by the dour-faced Miss Jauntley, the department's assistant manager.

'I'd say the crowd's bigger than we had last month for Liz,' Miss Jauntley observed.

'*Liz?*' Brandon repeated. 'As in Taylor?'

'Well, certainly. Can you think of another?'

True enough, Brandon thought. Liz was Liz and didn't need a last name anymore, just as for all these women (and, Brandon noticed, a scattering of dewy-eyed, feverishly hormonal junior-high boys), it was just plain Nicole.

For the next hour-and-a-half, Brandon watched

admiringly as Nicole did her stuff. For each new supplicant, whether babbling or tongue-tied, there was a smile, eye contact, a few whispered words and a personalized autographed picture. And the whole time, the cash registers just kept ringing and ringing.

How long has it been since Liz made a movie? he wrote in his notebook. *And of course Nicole has yet to make a film or appear on TV, except the occasional talk show. Why do models like Nicole get all this adulation? Are their names in the gossip columns really enough?*

What does fame really mean if it's not attached to real accomplishment? Celebrity just happens, it doesn't have to have a reason!

So is it worth it? Is it worth having the tabloids make up scandalous stories about you and having your private life laid out for everybody to see?

He looked up from his writing: The queues of people moved forward without cease, the fans just kept coming and coming, and Nicole just went on smiling and chatting and inscribing, like some beautiful automaton.

Nicole works very, very hard at this fame business. Up at dawn, she'll be going until after midnight, her press agent tells me. And this is a typical day! But is it really worth it?

She's our age, and already she's a total pro. But at what price?

*

Lunch was at Jimmy's, for years *the* show-business power-lunch eatery in that part of town, or so Max informed him as they limo'd the few blocks from the shopping centre.

In the wood-panelled anteroom, another tuxedo'd *maitre d'* wordlessly handed Brandon a clip-on tie. 'Just a formality. For the comfort of our guests,' he intoned.

Even Brandon, who prided himself on ignoring such things, recognized many of the diners in the room: movie stars, TV celebrities, famous and powerful Hollywood moguls. It was a seen-it-all, jaded crowd. Nevertheless, a ripple of excitement and covert glances followed them as they crossed the dining room to their corner table.

Two tables away, Samantha Sanders, Steve's TV-star mother, held court.

A tall, distinguished-looking, grey-haired man in a double-breasted pinstriped suit detached himself from Samantha's group and strolled casually over to Nicole.

'Hi, sweetheart,' he said, bending and kissing her on both cheeks. 'Max, old man. Roland, nice to see you again . . .' His noncommittal gaze fell on Brandon. 'A new beau, Nicole?'

Her laugh was easy and musical. 'A student from West Beverly, here to write about me for the school newspaper. Brandon Walsh, this is Stanley Morris, my agent.'

'Merely her movie and television agent,' Stanley said, shaking Brandon's hand. To Nicole he added as he took a seat, 'Darling, I should have known you wouldn't be dating boys your own age.'

'Oh, I don't know, Stanley.' Nicole gave Brandon a coquettish look. 'I just might surprise you.'

'Well, my dear, I have some surprises for you, too. *Offers*, lots of offers.'

And for the next hour Stanley regaled them with the possibilities. To Brandon, it seemed as if every director he'd ever heard of wanted Nicole to play an *ingenue* role in his next picture. But Nicole just picked at her chicken salad, sipped more champagne, chain-smoked and rejected them all.

'But, dear,' the agent said at last. 'What *is* it you want?'

'Oh, I will know it when it comes,' she replied, absentmindedly twirling a strand of her auburn hair around one finger. 'Not something big, Stanley, where I'll attract the critical attention. I want to have the long career, so we start out small. A supporting role, not the female lead; something where I can *act*, not decorate the set.'

Brandon was impressed. Stanley just held out his hands, palms up, and shrugged. 'You know what's best, my darling,' he conceded.

Just before they got up to leave, Nicole took out a small jewelled case, carefully removed two pills and swallowed them with the last of her champagne.

'Vitamins,' she said sweetly, seeing the look of concern on Brandon's face.

Chapter Nine

'We're spinnin' noon tunes for all you West Beverly rap-lovin' dudes . . .

'Yes, yes, yes! It's WBHS on the air again!'

David's amplified voice blasted through loudspeakers outside school and rumbled across the wide expanse of green lawn.

'And this is your A1 D.J., Diamond Dave!'

David Singer might be a geeky, nasal-voiced freshman the rest of the time, but inside the school radio station's glass-walled control booth, he was Rap Master Dave, the Man in Charge. But, as usual, he went too far.

And, as usual, Scott – his Lakers cap, worn backwards, covering his unruly mop of blond hair – was in the booth with him, egging him on.

'Yes, yes, yes, boys and girls, dudes and dude-ettes, you're gonna hear all your fave raves! But first, right here on WBHS, another episode of that ever-popular soap opera, "As West Beverly Turns"! . . .'

Outside, knots of students had gathered as they did

everyday during lunch – eating, tossing frisbees, throwing footballs, or just working on their tans.

Dylan strode purposefully across the lawn. His shades, black T-shirt and jeans, the long coat flapping behind him – it all said, don't mess with me.

He looked up. A hundred feet ahead, sitting in the shade of a spreading Coast Live Oak, was Brenda. Dylan stopped dead.

From the loudspeakers came David's irritating amplified whine:

'Yes, yes, yes! In our last episode, the dread French Rival had returned to the hills of Beverly! Who will she fall for now? . . .

'The old boyfriend? But wait! There's a new guy in the picture! The old boyfriend has a new girlfriend, and she has a brother! . . .

'One of Diamond Dave's many spies just returned from an unauthorized visit to Century City, and what did he see? . . .'

Dylan was on the move, reacting not so much to D.J. Dave's words as to the stricken look on Brenda's face. He rushed up the steps, taking them two at a time, not even registering the presence of Andrea. She, too, was frozen, that same horrified and hurt look on *her* face.

Once inside, he ran flat out down the hallway, sliding around a corner, bumping into three startled co-eds, side-stepping a spluttering teacher, skidding around another corner, nearly falling on the waxed floor, then sprinting the last few yards . . .

'Yes, yes, yes! You saw her on the cover of Vogue, *you saw her on the cover of* Elle, *you saw her in the* National Enquirer, *and now she'll be on the cover of West Beverly's own award-winning newspaper! . . .*

'But has our muckraking reporter gotten too close to

his subject? Have the Parisian Girl's charms claimed another victim? . . .'

Dylan came crashing through the control-booth door, knocking over a cassette-laden cart. The two freshman sat bolt upright, staring at him in wide-eyed fright.

Over the outdoor loudspeakers came two high-pitched squeaks, then a single bellowed word:

'TWERPS!!!'

Reflexively, the students outside looked up at the loudspeakers.

'Yikes! Hey, man, you can't—'

There was a staticky crackle, then a high-pitched electronic whine, then . . . silence.

The students on the lawn gave a collective shrug, then someone threw a frisbee and they all carried on with their various lunch hour pursuits.

Chapter Ten

As the afternoon wore on, they motored East, into Hollywood. They turned North off Sunset at Highland, a busy intersection dominated by a complex of greying stucco and red-tile roofed buildings.

'That's Hollywood High,' Max said, 'and right across the street, where that mini-mall is now, that used to be Schwab's.'

'Schwab's?' Nicole repeated.

'Yeah, Schwab's drugstore. It used to be really famous back in the Thirties and Forties. You heard of Rita Hayworth?'

'*Oui.*'

'Well, the story goes, she was a student right there at Hollywood High, and one day she went across the street for a soda. She was sitting at the counter when a talent scout discovered her. The rest, as they say, is history.

'Kinda reminds me of you, honey,' Max continued. 'You know, discovered in high school and all.' Max snapped his fingers. 'Hey, I just got an idea. Roland, what do you say we put Nicole in one of those sexy sheath kinda dresses Rita used to wear, take some snaps, send it to *People*. Bet they run it.'

Nicole gave Brandon an ironic smile, as if to say, What can I do, it's part of what's required of me.

They only had a few blocks to go, but they were caught in traffic, so Max rambled on. 'You know, you remind me of Rita in another way. After she became a big star and everything, she fell for this playboy-type guy.'

Nicole gave him a sharp look, but he continued on obliviously. 'Not that I believe everything I read in the tabs. Hell, I plant half that stuff myself. But anyway, I think it was back in the summer of '48. Rita was in the South of France, waiting for her divorce from Orson Welles to come through, and she meets this Aly Khan guy. Real rich, some kinda hereditary Muslim prophet, too. Descended from Muhammad, that kinda thing. Anyway, Rita was under contract to Columbia at the time, and they didn't take kindly to this romance stuff. So even though she was, like, the biggest star in the world by then, Columbia suspended her.

'I remember one of the trade papers ran this famous headline. Let's see, what was it?' Max stared up at the limo ceiling for a moment to jog his memory. 'Oh yeah, the guy who canned her was Harry Cohn, a real crusty sorta old-timey guy. So anyway, this was the headline: "From Cohn to Cannes to Khan to Canned". What a hoot!'

*

Their first stop was a great, weathered lime green building on the corner of Hollywood and Highland that had once housed the Max Factor company. It still contained a cosmetics museum on the ground floor, but the upper storeys were now the world headquarters of the skin-care products conglomerate that manufactured Parisian Girl Perfume.

Nicole, of course, got the royal, returning-prodigal-daughter treatment, escorted around the museum and the company offices by none other than the president of the whole conglomerate himself, while Roland danced ahead of them, shooting roll after roll of film to memorialise the event. Max and Brandon trailed along behind the excited crowd of employees that followed Nicole's every move.

'Say, Max, tell me how this works. Nicole's the Parisian Girl, and she's in all those sexy perfume commercials you see on TV. You know, all that "Share the Fantasy" stuff. But she's a cover girl, too, right? And those magazine covers don't have anything to do with perfume.'

'Well, yes and no. It's all about selling, kid. The way it works is this: When Nicole's doin' a magazine shoot or she's modelling at one of those Parisian high-fashion things they have a couple of times a year, she gets top dollar. I'm talking *thousands* a day. Now, she can model for anybody, be on the cover of any magazine, and Parisian Girl Perfume's got nothing to say about it. Of course, there's a morals clause in her contract, so she can't do any of those skin magazines. Not that she'd want to, mind you, or that I'd let her even if she wanted to and could.'

'But the perfume guys pay her mega-bucks – I'm talking a million-five a year – to do their perfume ads and a few P.A.s like this morning—'

'P.A.?'

'Public appearance, kid. You sure you go to West Beverly? I thought all you guys were like CAA agents in training.'

Brandon laughed. 'I guess I'm still not your typical West Beverly student.'

'Oh yeah, I forgot. You come from fly-over country in the Midwest there. Anyway, the deal is, Nicole can't do any perfume ads for anybody else. There's even a clause that says a magazine can't run her picture on the facing page if there's another company's perfume ad opposite it. Typical stuff. Get it, kid?'

'I guess so,' Brandon said. He thought about it. 'Max?'

'Yeah, kid?'

'Aren't you worried about her?'

'*Worried?* About Nicole? That girl was born wised-up. What's to worry about?'

Brandon checked his watch. 'It's almost three o'clock. She hasn't eaten anything yet.'

Max chuckled dismissively. 'It's some metabolism thing. Besides, all these top super-model types don't eat. They're always dieting. I mean, listen kid, did I ever tell you about Marilyn Monroe?'

*

Celebrity is all about selling, Brandon wrote in his notebook, while Nicole smiled and posed her way through yet another photo shoot, this time with the company's assembled board of directors, *and sometimes it's all about selling out. Nicole Didier is wised-up (as her press agent puts it) alright; she's smart enough to turn down starring roles in movies, because the parts aren't right. But her day, which seems so glamorous from the outside, is filled with one inane event after another, all of which she has to take with the utmost seriousness and professionalism. And while the attitude is commendable, the activities are not. We're not talking about brain surgery or curing cancer or furthering world peace, after all. And the worst part of it, it seems to me, is the brutal, non-stop pace.*

*

'Oh, please, Max, just a quick stop. We have the few minutes, no?'

Brandon was amazed. One moment, she was the sharp-tongued mistress of her own career; the next, she was a little girl pleading with 'Uncle' Max to make a small detour to the red-and-gold Chinese pagoda she'd spotted on teeming Hollywood Boulevard.

What had so excited Nicole was the former Grauman's Chinese Theatre, now known as the Mann Chinese, where for decades stars had been memorialised with their hand and footprints in cement.

'Okay, I suppose we can spare a coupla minutes,' Max said gruffly, ordering the limo driver to 'pull up in front of the Chinese.'

'In front of the Japanese is more like it,' the driver muttered, so that only Brandon, in the jump seat, could hear him.

A minute later, Brandon understood what the driver had meant. The area in front of the venerable Chinese Theatre was crowded with Japanese tourists, who, Nikons and Sony camcorders in hand, poured off an unending succession of tour buses.

'Do not be afraid, *cher* Max,' Nicole said cheerfully, putting on the huge round sunglasses that covered half her face. As soon as the limo pulled up to the curb, she bounded out and waded happily into the crowd. Brandon, somewhat tentatively, stepped out and followed after her.

'*Ooh la-la!*' Nicole clapped her hands together with

glee. '*Regardez*, Marilyn's hands.' She pointed down at the concrete. 'How tiny! Did you not see the "Seven Year Itch"?' She twirled around so that her skirt rode high up on her long legs. '*Trés chic*.'

'Pardon please, Miss.' A middle-aged Japanese man held out a pad of paper and a pen. 'Kindly sign.'

And with that, a murmur washed over the densely packed tourists. From all directions the crowd surged, as sudden as a Midwestern thunderstorm; and at the eye of the storm, Nicole was shoved into Brandon's arms.

Someone he couldn't see lifted a camcorder over Brandon's shoulder and the heavy plastic edge clipped his cheek. Brandon swatted it away with his free hand, while holding Nicole tightly with the other.

'*S'il vous plait*. Please,' Nicole was saying, 'just move back and I will sign for everyone.'

But of course, most of the tourists didn't understand English, and those further back kept pressing towards her. The crush instantly grew tighter.

Nicole was in Brandon's arms, facing him, her head pressed against his chest. Slowly, with excruciating care, Brandon backed them both up, protecting her by taking the full force of the pressure himself.

The limousine – and safety – was twenty-five feet away; it seemed like twenty-five miles.

Slowly, slowly, he edged back. From the crowd's second rank, a hand blindly waving a metal-point pen cut the air an inch from Nicole's million-dollar face. Brandon batted it down.

Curious passersby, seeing the *mêlée*, stopped to gawk and pressed inwards, adding to the throng, which suddenly surged again. This time, they nearly went down.

Only the human wall, pushing in on them, kept them from falling.

Three feet.

Five feet.

Will power gave Brandon strength. He continued to push against them.

Six feet. Seven . . .

Nicole's sunglasses were askew and Brandon could see the stark terror in her eyes.

From somewhere in the back of the crowd, a woman screamed.

Eight feet. Nine . . . Ten.

A fight between two of the tourists broke out next to them. Brandon parried the wild blows.

He risked a look over his shoulder. Through the seething tangle of arms and legs, he glimpsed Roland, Max and the uniformed limo driver. They were fighting their way towards them.

The limo driver had placed himself strategically. His fists flew and the crowd parted in confusion. Suddenly, Roland was there, and he snatched Nicole from Brandon's protective grasp.

Just as quickly as it had begun, the peril was ended. Somehow, they were back in the limo and the driver was behind the wheel.

'Hammer it!' Max growled, and the driver pressed the accelerator to the floor.

'Are you okay, dear?' In Roland's voice was deep concern.

'Yes,' she said tremulously, gazing wide-eyed at Brandon. 'But you are hurt.'

A thin trickle of blood descended from the nick on his cheek. 'It's nothing,' he said.

'*Au contraire*,' she said, gently wiping the blood off with a silk handkerchief. 'I do believe you've saved my life.'

By the time they reached the Sheraton Hotel in

Universal City, just over the Cahuenga Pass from Hollywood, Nicole was totally composed. She was, after all, about to go to work again, modelling at a charity fashion show.

'Have you ever attended a fashion show?' Nicole asked.

'Uh-uh.'

'Then you should view this one from the backstage,' she said giggling.

At the time, Brandon didn't understand the sharp looks both Max and Roland shot her simultaneously.

A few minutes later though, as he sat in a stiff-backed chair in the models' changing room, his face flushing red with embarrassment, Brandon knew.

The room was filled with beautiful young women in beautiful *haute couture* clothes . . . clothes that they kept taking off as they rushed back from the catwalk to change.

Brandon didn't know where to look, surrounded as he was by these leggy creatures throwing thousand-dollar dresses over clothes racks, dabbing on make-up, shrugging into another dress and racing back out, all to the beat of pounding rap music that drifted backstage.

Nicole, wearing a skintight, beaded red minidress came speeding back. An assistant unzipped her and Nicole stepped out of the expensive dress, letting it fall to the floor.

She was wearing a white silk teddy, stockings and high heels. 'You like?' she asked innocently, smiling over at him.

'Oh, indeed, yes, very much,' Brandon babbled, unable to take his eyes off her as the dresser helped her slip into a black cocktail dress. 'Oh, oh, the dress. Yes, very much. Nice, uh, dress . . .'

Nicole laughed, tossed her hair and sashayed away.

Chapter Eleven

Brenda eased herself behind the wheel of the battered old car she and her brother shared. Crossing the street in front of her was Andrea.

To Brenda, she seemed to be walking a little slower, clutching her schoolbooks a little tighter.

Poor Andrea, Brenda thought. *She's depressed.* She sighed. *But so am I.*

Brenda thought a moment, then got out of the car and walked over to where Andrea was sitting.

'Hi.'

'Hi, Brenda.'

'Whatcha doing?'

Andrea shrugged, looked around as if to point out how silly a question it was. 'Waiting for the bus. Going home.'

Brenda laughed nervously. 'Want to come over?'

Andrea tilted her head back, giving Brenda an appraising look. Sunlight glinted off her glasses. 'Come over,' she repeated. 'Why?'

'Oh, I don't know. I thought maybe we could study a while together. You know, just hang out, wait for

Brandon to get back. Maybe we could all go down to the Peach Pit.'

'Wait for Brandon to get back?' Andrea repeated tartly. 'Go down to the Peach Pit?'

'C'mon, Andrea, there's no need for sarcasm.'

'Or for pity,' Andrea snapped.

Brenda wasn't easily cowed, not even by the formidable school-paper editor. She put her hands on her hips, feeling momentarily just like her mother. 'Cut that out, Andrea. Did you ever stop and think that just maybe this is a case of misery wanting company? If there's anyone around here who's pitiful, it's . . .' All of a sudden, her lower lip was trembling, 'me.'

Andrea took a deep breath and sighed. 'I'm sorry, Brenda. It's just that ever since that dumb disc jockey . . . Well, all afternoon, I've felt like I was a character in some teenage version of "Peyton Place". With everybody whispering kind of just out of earshot and everything.'

Brenda laughed nervously, but felt relief. 'I know exactly what you mean.'

'Well, at least you didn't throw your boyfriend at that, that French bimbo.'

Brenda snorted. 'Hah! If you only knew! . . . Well, you coming?'

Andrea smiled. 'Sure. Let's go "study".'

*

The hands of the kitchen wall clock moved with infuriating slowness. Andrea and Brenda were at the table, half-eaten sandwiches pushed aside, their books spread out before them. Andrea's elbow was on the table and her chin rested in her cupped hand. She turned a page desultorily. 'What time is it?'

Brenda looked up. 'Same time it was when you asked last time . . . only five minutes later . . . Ten to seven.'

'Oh.' Andrea sighed. She adjusted her glasses and tried to focus on her book.

Brenda's mother breezed in from the living room, carrying two empty coffee cups. 'Refills,' she announced brightly, going over to the pot on the counter. 'At this rate, Jim and I are going to be up half the night. Hope there's something good on the late show.'

'It's "Gorilla of my Dreams" week, Mrs. Walsh,' Andrea said in a monotone. 'I think it's "Son of Kong" tonight.'

Cindy Walsh put the cups down carefully, turned and put her hands on her hips, exactly the way Brenda had at the bus stop. 'Whatever's the matter with the two of you? I've seen happier faces at funerals.'

'It's nothing, Mom,' Brenda said. 'Homework's kinda boring, that's all.'

Cindy Walsh knew better than to pry. ' "Son of Kong", huh? Unfortunately, that sounds just like the kind of movie Jim would stay up to see.'

'Brandon, too,' Andrea said.

'Like father like son,' Brenda's mother replied as the kitchen flew open and Brandon fairly burst in. 'Well, speak of the devil.'

'Hi, Mom . . . Hi, Brenda . . . Hi, Andrea.' Brandon looked too excited to stand still. He was carrying something in a plastic bag draped over his shoulder.

'What's that, dear?'

'Oh, um, nothin', Mom.' Brandon shifted his weight nervously. 'Just a tux.'

'A tux?' Brenda repeated incredulously. 'You don't own a tuxedo.'

'It's, uh, rented. We, um, stopped off at Tuxedo

Centre on the way back from Universal City. Um, ah, I need it to go to the première tonight.'

'*Première?*' all three women repeated at once.

For the first time Brandon looked in Andrea's direction. 'It's, ah, turning into a longer assignment than I thought. But don't worry,' he added in a rush. 'I'm going to get a really good piece out of it.'

Andrea's eyes narrowed. 'I'll bet you are,' she said in a clipped tone.

'Well, uh . . .' Brandon was edging past them. 'I, uh, gotta shower and get dressed. The, uh, limo's going to be here in a half hour to pick me up.'

'The limo?' Cindy Walsh sounded impressed. 'My, how fancy!'

'Oh, yeah, well . . .' Brandon waved a hand dismissively. 'It's, uh, nothing, really.'

'Dear?'

Brandon had almost made it out of the room. 'Yes, Mom?'

'How did you get that scratch on your face?'

Brandon touched the small mark on his cheek. 'Oh. That. Well, uh . . . Somebody bumped into me. It's, uh, nothing. Really.'

Under her breath, Andrea said, 'It looks like a hickey to me.'

But Brandon was already out the door and halfway up the steps.

Brenda and Andrea exchanged a look. It was a look that women from time immemorial had been giving each other. It was both a look of sympathy and a what-did-you-expect-he's-a-man look.

'Not him too,' Brenda sighed. 'We could steal the tux while he's in the shower, or maybe trip him when he's coming down the stairs. If we're lucky, he'll break a leg or something.'

'Girls?'

'Oh, Mom, it's nothing,' Brenda said, mimicking her brother. '*Really.*'

'It's just not worth it,' Andrea declared, getting up and closing her books. 'I'm going home.'

'Wait up,' Brenda said. 'I'll drive you.'

*

It hadn't started out as a spying mission. Not really. It just turned out that way.

All Andrea wanted to do was go home, take a hot bath and have herself a good mope.

And all Brenda wanted to do was get out of the house and forget about her own troubles for a while.

But there was Andrea's Big Secret to consider, a secret that both Brenda and Brandon shared:

Andrea Zuckerman attended West Beverly High illegally. She didn't actually live in the West Beverly school district; she just used her grandmother's Beverly Hills condominium as a mailing address, so she could attend the prestigious high school, which had the kind of academic reputation that attracted Ivy League scouts.

Andrea's real home was in a modest, somewhat shabby residential neighbourhood in the shadow of the Hollywood hills.

So it *wasn't* premeditated. They really *did* intend to go straight to Andrea's. But as they drove down seedy Santa Monica Boulevard, they couldn't help noticing the searchlights criss-crossing against the night sky.

They both knew what those beams meant; in Hollywood, gala premières were weekly events.

'Humph,' Andrea huffed.

'Really,' Brenda agreed.

They drove on in silence. As they went further East, traffic slowed to a crawl.

'I'm getting off this,' Brenda said, manoeuvring into the turning lane.

'You could take Sunset,' Andrea advised.

'Yeah, I suppose.'

They headed North, towards the hills. Brenda drove with one hand while she fiddled with the radio, trying to find some music she liked.

'Of all the nerve,' Brenda muttered. 'I mean, my own brother.'

'Men,' Andrea said with disgust.

'Yeah,' Brenda agreed.

They shot through a busy intersection on the tail end of a yellow light.

'You passed it,' Andrea said.

'What?'

'That was Sunset.'

'Oh . . . I could go Franklin.'

Ahead and to their right, the searchlights swept the sky. They looked like hands beckoning, Brenda thought.

'You could go Hollywood, I suppose,' said Andrea, casually.

'Yeah, we could,' Brenda replied. 'We could check out the sights.'

At the last second, she turned abruptly East again, only busy Hollywood Boulevard. Dead ahead, the searchlights crossed and crossed again.

*

Nicole didn't just look great, she was breathtaking. This time, she and Brandon were alone in the limo's back seat.

She had on a shimmery black mini-dress, backless, with a plunging neckline. Diamonds decorated her ears, hung around her long neck and twinkled at the points of her spike-heeled shoes. Even her stockings sparkled with light.

'It's kind of funny coming back to the Mann's Chinese,' Brandon said, tugging at the tight wing collar of his formal shirt. 'I mean, after what happened there this afternoon.'

'This time, you will see, it will be different. Very many *gendarmes* between us and the admiring public.'

Brandon laughed nervously. 'I've never been to one of these première things before.'

Nicole put a hand on his knee. 'You will enjoy, Brandon. I promise.'

'I'm sure.'

'Champagne?' She poured herself another glass.

'No, no thanks. I don't drink anymore.'

'As you wish, *mon cher*.'

Nicole snapped her small silver handbag open. She took out the jewelled pillbox, picked out two gelatin capsules, popped them in her mouth and swallowed.

'Vitamins?' Brandon's eyebrow arched.

'But of course.' Nicole smiled.

Brandon took a deep breath. He gave the glittering vision as level a gaze as he could, under the circumstances, summon. 'Aren't you going to offer me any of those, uh, "vitamins"?'

'You would like?' She held out the jewelled case.

'No. I would *not* like,' Brandon replied. 'It's just that y'know, I'm this Minnesota guy, but I've been at West Beverly a while now, and I thought the etiquette rule was, if you've got drugs, you offer to share.'

Nicole's smile was dazzling, but Brandon could see it was merely a reflex. Professional. Frozen.

'Drugs?' she repeated, as if she were hearing the word for the first time.

'Yeah, your "vitamins". Don't you think I've seen capsules like that before? Red and blue. They're amphetamines, right? Diet pills.

'Hell, Nicole, I've been tagging along with you this whole crazy day. You haven't eaten enough to keep a hummingbird alive. And you've been downing the bubbly since this morning.

'You seem like a really sweet girl, but you've got a problem. A *serious* problem.'

Nicole just continued to stare at him, that same smile fixed on her beautiful face.

'So,' she said at last. 'I thank you for your comments, Brandon, but the problem now is all this.' She waved in the direction of the theatre just ahead.

Brandon peered out of the limo window. The crowd at the theatre with the pagoda facade dwarfed by far the mob of tourists they'd encountered that afternoon. It spilled out into the street, squeezing traffic on busy Hollywood boulevard to just two slow-moving lines of cars filled with gawking passersby. Police on horseback patrolled the perimeter. A double line of wooden barricades kept open a red-carpeted lane for the arriving celebrities.

The limousine glided up to the theatre entrance. A tuxedo'd functionary with a walkie-talkie held open the limo door. Brandon stepped out, turned and offered Nicole his hand.

As soon as the crowd got its first glimpse of leggy, glamorous Nicole, a tremendous roar went up and Brandon was almost blinded by the electric blizzard of flashing lights.

The red-carpeted lane bristled with TV cameras and microphones. Reporters shouted questions that went unheard in the cacophony. As they moved arm-in-arm toward the entranceway, Brandon scanned the crowd.

From the corner of his eye, he thought he glimpsed his sister and Andrea in the seething sea of humanity. But a flashbulb went off right in his face. The blinding white light washed away the incongruous sight.

Naw, he thought to himself, *it couldn't be.*

*

'I know he's my brother and everything,' Brenda was saying as they drove off into the neon-tinted night, 'but *how* could Brandon make such a spectacle of himself?'

'He really looked good in his tuxedo,' Andrea remarked wistfully.

Brenda giggled. 'Did you hear what that lady in the baggy shorts said when we were leaving?'

'No. Which one?'

'The one with the varicose veins and knobbly knees. She was carrying this ratty-looking poodle and standing next to me when we were waiting at the corner to cross at the lights?'

'Uh-uh.'

'She thought Brandon was Tom Cruise. She wanted his autograph. So I said that was my brother, and then she wanted *my* autograph.'

This time, they both giggled. 'You should've given it to her,' Andrea remarked.

The absurdity of it all lightened their moods. 'You don't really want to go straight home, do you?' Brenda asked.

Andrea thought about it. Moping didn't seem like such a good idea, after all. 'Welllll . . . I suppose not, but I sure don't want to stick around Hollywood Boulevard. It really gets weird there late at night.'

'So what should we do? Go to a club? Call Donna and Kelly? Cruise Sunset?'

'No, I don't think I'm in the mood for any of that.'

'I've got it,' Brenda said. 'Let's drop by the Peach Pit and drown our sorrows in a Diet Coke.'

CHAPTER TWELVE

'Did you enjoy it, Brandon?' Nicole asked in a tiny voice, breaking the silence that had descended on their limo ride.

She sat across from him in the back seat, her long legs crossed, hands folded demurely in her lap. She looked, Brandon thought, lovely . . . and sad.

'Sure,' Brandon said, without much conviction. He unknotted his bow tie and unfastened the top button of his uncomfortably tight dress shirt. 'Whew, that's better.

'It was really exciting and all – you know, all those fans shouting your name, that noise, the cameras and the lights, the stars and stuff. Who wouldn't like something like that?'

He yawned. 'Boy, it's been a really long day. I don't know how you do it.' Brandon smiled wearily. 'Well, actually, I *do* know how you do it . . .'

'My "vitamins"?'

'Your *speed*,' he corrected, leaning intently towards her. He covered her hands with his own. 'Listen, Nicole,

I like you a lot. It's not just that you're beautiful. You're really smart and, and . . . you're *nice*.

'You're a genuinely good person, and you're working yourself to death!

'That's why you *must* do something about this! You must do something about this, this . . . addiction.'

'But Brandon, I *need* them, I need them just to get through the day. Sometimes, I'm so tired . . .'

'Those are *amphetamines* you're taking! They're dangerous, Nicole, you know that as well as I do.'

'Yes,' she said softly. 'I know they are not vitamins. They are diet pills, amphetamines. It's right.'

'Good. Admitting that is a start.'

'But, Brandon,' she sighed. 'So many people depend on me. I have so much responsibility.'

'What about your child?'

'*Oui*. More than anything, I do this for her.'

'*No*,' Brandon exclaimed heatedly. 'You're smarter than that. That's just a rationalisation. It's for her that you must *stop* doing this. You must stop for yourself . . .'

'But I don't think it's possible. The days are too full, the nights are too long . . .'

'Listen, Nicole, you're young now; young and healthy and strong. But that stuff takes its toll.

'The longer you wait, the harder it's going to be. The longer you wait, the more damage you risk.'

He was reaching her, Brandon was certain. The professional poise, the polished smile were gone. Her lower lip trembled, a single tear coursed down her flawless cheek.

He reached over and brushed the tear away. 'You can stop, you can do it, you can take control again.'

She leaned her head against him; he put his arm around her shoulders.

'What can I do?' she whispered. 'What can I do?'

'You're starting to do it already. You're admitting to yourself that there *is* a problem. That's the first step.

'And you're admitting to yourself that those pills aren't "vitamins", they're drugs. That's good too.'

'But what should I do? What should I do now?'

Brandon took the jewelled pillbox and placed it in her open hand. 'Throw these out the window. Just do it. Then, in the morning, call your doctor, in Paris if you have to, and find a good clinic, a rehab centre, where they can help you kick the habit.

'Then come back, take care of your baby, live your life, and don't let Max or anybody else schedule every minute of your day. That's an insane way to live.'

Nicole looked down at the pillbox; it winked seductively with reflective light.

Nicole straightened, pushed away from him. She closed her hand tightly around the little box. 'No, Brandon, I cannot. Not yet.'

'*Nicole . . .*'

She hushed him with a scarlet-tipped finger to his lips. 'I must think for a time . . .'

She smiled. The poised model with an adoring world at her feet was back. 'Perhaps, *cheri*, you could *help* me think.'

'I'll help you in any way that I can,' Brandon said earnestly.

'Then come back with me to my hotel. We'll drink champagne and talk.' She gave him a bold, unmistakeable look. 'You can spend the night.'

Brandon flushed crimson. The lurid possibilities flashed through his mind. He imagined Steve Sanders and his cronies congratulating him and slapping him on the back. *No*, he couldn't, he *mustn't*.

He forced himself to realize that it was the drugs and the alcohol talking, not Nicole. Still . . .

He took a deep breath. 'I'm flattered, *very* flattered,' he said. 'But I can't. It wouldn't be right.'

'*Pourquoi?*'

'For lots of reasons . . . Dylan, my sister, my girlfriend, your kid. Besides, you're not straight; I'd be taking advantage. And you've got to get up early again, I'll bet, and start this craziness all over.'

Nicole wasn't exactly familiar with rejection, and she didn't take it well. 'As you wish, Brandon,' she said stiffly. 'The driver will take you to your house.'

Brandon shook his head. 'No, there's this place I work at back in the real world. The Peach Pit. It's a little coffee shop not far from here. I should stop in and help Matt close up.'

CHAPTER THIRTEEN

It was a school night, it was late. But the Peach Pit was packed, and Donna and Kelly were there. So Brenda and Andrea joined them at a booth by the front window.

And getting together with Donna and Kelly meant rapid-fire, non-stop exchange of gossip.

'Steve Sanders was here,' Donna began in an insinuating tone. 'He said he ran into Dylan, and Dylan was *very* eager to find out where Nicole was staying tonight.'

'Terrific,' Brenda said glumly.

'*Very* eager,' Donna repeated, just in case Brenda hadn't got the point. 'But we thought it was *trés* strange that he had to actually ask Steve.'

'I don't get it,' Andrea interjected. 'What's Steve got to do with it?'

'Well, you know Steve,' Kelly replied. 'He got his mommy to ask her agent.'

'What a sweet guy,' Andrea said archly.

'Yeah, really, I don't know what I ever saw in the

guy,' Kelly replied thoughtfully. 'I suppose it was the Corvette. Anyway, Steve doesn't do anything for anybody unless there's something in it for him.'

'I guess that's why he dated you all last year,' Andrea said as sweetly as she knew how.

Kelly ignored the dig. 'Be that as it may, we all know I can still twist the guy around my little finger.'

Kelly held up the finger in question, pausing for dramatic effect.

'So?' Andrea prompted.

'So, I got him to tell me.'

Again, she paused a beat.

'*So?*' Andrea repeated. 'What did he tell you?'

'So he told me what he got out of it. He said he made Dylan promise to fix him up with Nicole.'

Kelly fixed Brenda with her best I'm-gazing-into-your-soul look. 'Well, Brenda, what do you think about *that*?'

Brenda was about to tell both of them *exactly* what she thought about that, when a long black limousine pulled silently up to the curb outside.

'Well, will you look at that!' Donna exclaimed. 'A stretch limo at the Peach Pit!'

Andrea didn't want to look, but she couldn't turn away either, not when everyone else in the Pit was staring outside.

She watched, heart suddenly pounding in her chest, as a uniformed chauffeur, dressed all in black, came around and held open the curbside door.

Brandon, resplendent in his tuxedo, stepped out. Then, in cruel pantomime, a willowly arm and a long leg appeared. Brandon held out his hand.

It had become so quiet in the normally noisy Peach Pit that, even through the pane of glass, Andrea and the others could hear.

'Please think about it,' Brandon was saying. 'You've got to make the right decision.'

'I will, my dear.'

The glittering vision stood on tiptoe, very close to him, and kissed him, once, lightly on the cheek. Then she was gone.

Donna broke the silence. '*Wow!*'

*

Matt, who'd been flipping burgers on the grill, was probably the only one in the Pit not to witness the brief tableau.

He turned, wiping his hands on his apron, to find his best part-time waiter strolling up, dressed to the nines in a tuxedo.

'Hey, Minnesota,' he called out. 'Who died and left you the monkey suit?'

Brandon grinned crookedly. 'Don't worry, boss, it's rented.'

A puzzled frown fixed itself on Matt's placid face. 'Hey, hows come it's so quiet in here?' he bellowed, going to the register and ringing up 'no sale'. He grabbed a handful of quarters and dropped them in Brandon's palm. 'Go ahead, Brandon, play some of your favourite tunes. This one time, it's on the house.'

Brandon gave him a mock salute. 'You got it, boss man. Anything special you want to hear?'

' "She Drives Me Crazy",' Matt said instantly. 'Those Fine Young Cannibals are, well, really fine.'

Brandon chuckled. 'Better watch out, Matt, I think you're in danger of getting too hip.'

He sauntered over to the vintage jukebox, put in the money and began pressing buttons.

It was only when the driving beat of Matt's favourite

song began that Brandon turned, scanned the faces at the packed little restaurant and finally noticed Brenda and Andrea there.

'Hi, guys,' he said jauntily, walking over to their booth. 'Mind if I join you?'

'Why?' Donna replied waspishly. 'Are we coming apart?'

'Hah-hah-hah!' Brandon snorted. 'Aren't we Miss Wit tonight?'

Miss Half Wit, Andrea might have added under other circumstances, but not tonight. 'Actually, we were just leaving, Brandon,' she said as coldly as she could. She stood up. 'Coming, Brenda?'

'Yeah, right.' Standing up, Brenda shot her brother an angry glance. 'I'll be home soon.'

'Hey, what about me?' A confused, forlorn note had crept into Brandon's voice. 'Are you just going to leave me here?'

'I'm sure one of your many admirers will be just delighted to drive you anywhere you want to go,' Brenda snapped.

'That's right,' Andrea added as the two girls marched out shoulder-to-shoulder. 'You can always tell them you're Tom Cruise.'

'Huh?' Brandon stared after them in open-mouthed amazement. 'What did I do?'

Deflated, he collapsed into the booth, opposite Donna and Kelly. 'What's gotten into those two?' he asked.

Kelly patted his hand in a parody of solicitousness. 'Don't you worry about a thing, stud. One of these days you'll understand.'

'Men!' Donna snorted, rolling her eyes skywards.

*

‘ “It was a dark and stormy night” . . .’

‘Huh?’ Steve Sanders, behind the wheel of his parked Corvette convertible with its 184RE customised license plate, looked over at Dylan McKay as if he were crazy. He leaned back and gazed up into the cloudless, starry night sky. ‘What’re you talking about? It’s nice out.’

Dylan shook his head. ‘It’s nothing, Steve, just a famous line of melodramatic bad writing.’

‘ “Melodramatic bad writing”? Whew, McKay you’re getting weird.’

‘I guess I was just thinking about those two freshmen – Scott and David or whatever their names are – on the radio today.

‘I mean, maybe I overreacted, y’know. I mean, maybe they had a point with that soap opera stuff they were doing.

‘It’s like everybody’s been so wrapped up in this Nicole thing.

‘Me too, y’know. She shows up, and I freak. No wonder Brenda got so upset.’

‘Yeah, man, babes – who can figure ’em?’ Steve opined.

‘Naw, Sanders, that’s not what I’m talking about. She had a right. You know what I mean? I should’ve just taken care of business, had a quiet talk with Nicole, found out what’s what, what’s true and what’s just rumour and gossip.’

‘Yeah, man, I’m wondering if it’s just rumour that this Nicole babe of yours is ever going to show.’

They were sitting in the hillside parking lot just down from the Beverly Hills Hotel’s canopied front entrance. Steve had pressed a five-dollar bill into a parking attendant’s hand, and they’d been allowed to wait. And wait. And wait . . .

Steve checked his watch. 'It's getting late. Maybe we should come back tomorrow?'

'What if there is *no* tomorrow?' Dylan replied with what Steve took to be his usual sense of mystery.

'Yeah, right. Then I suppose classes will be cancelled, too.'

'You can go if you want. I'm staying.'

'Think she'll show?'

'Sooner or later.' Dylan yawned. 'When I knew her, a couple of years ago, that girl could party all night.'

'Yeah, well, that sounds *mucho* good to me. But it's later already, man, as far as I'm concerned.' Steve thought it over a moment. 'I really want to meet this babe, but the thing is I'm exhausted. I'm gonna book.'

'Whatever. But if you split, you might blow your chance. Fair warning.' Dylan didn't feel the need to mention *specifically* that he'd checked with a hotel clerk, who'd told him that Miss Didier and her party would be checking out in the morning.

'Yeah, fair warning,' Steve agreed. 'You tried to deliver, man.'

Dylan got out of the car slowly and stretched, taking a deep breath of the jasmine-scented night air.

'Want a ride back to your Porsche?'

'Nah,' Dylan replied. 'I'll just hang in the lobby a while, then catch a taxi back to my ride.'

'Whatever.' Steve switched on the ignition and the Corvette's powerful engine roared to life. 'Later.'

'Later.'

Dylan turned away and trudged back up the hill. As the taillights of the Corvette disappeared behind him, Dylan was caught in the twin beams of a limousine approaching the hotel from the other direction.

At last, he thought, Nicole!

CHAPTER FOURTEEN

'Don't children in Beverly Hills *ever* sleep?' Cindy Walsh asked, peering through the kitchen window at Dylan's familiar black Porsche parked outside. The street was quiet and peaceful in the early-morning light.

'What's that, honey?' Jim Walsh, setting off on yet another business trip, was fumbling with his paisley tie as he came in from the living room. 'God, I hate having to get on another airplane. It seems like I just got back from Chicago.'

'That's because you just did, dear.' She gave him a quick peck on the cheek and took the ends of the tie in her own dextrous hands. 'Here let me,' she said, looping it expertly.

'What's that about the children?'

'I got up around four to get a glass of water and the lights were on in both their rooms. And now Dylan's outside in his car, waiting for Brenda, I suppose.'

Jim Walsh peered down at his watch and frowned. 'It's not even seven yet. What's that boy up to anyway?'

'Why don't we invite him in, dear?'

'I don't know. I still wonder if I wasn't right about Dylan McKay the first time.'

Cindy sighed. She well remembered how suspicious her husband had been of Dylan when he and Brenda had first started dating. Dylan had won him over, but seeing his only daughter's boyfriend turning up as the 'mystery lover' in a gossipy tabloid story about some jet-setting European model hadn't exactly made him feel secure about Brenda's choice.

For that matter, it had caused Cindy some private qualms, too. 'Jim, I think in the final analysis we have no choice but to trust Brenda's judgment about this boy. We can't depend on gossip-mongers to form our opinion.'

'Yeah, you're right,' Jim conceded, and Cindy smiled. 'But I'd feel a lot more comfortable about it if one of us sat Brenda down and talked this out.'

'All in good time. Being a teenager these days isn't easy under the best of circumstances.'

'It seems it's especially hard in Beverly Hills,' Jim said gruffly. 'I don't know how adults would handle this kind of media attention, much less kids.'

'She knows we're here for her,' Cindy said, putting her arms affectionately around her husband's neck. 'It's obvious she's sorting out her feelings too.'

Jim wrapped his arms around his wife's waist and gave her a quick kiss. 'When did you get to be so smart?'

'When I married you, of course,' Cindy replied.

Jim Walsh laughed with pleasure. 'Okay, dear, you win. I'll go out and invite young Mr McKay in.'

*

Brenda, wearing a striped halter dress over a white blouse, was in the bathroom, fixing her make-up, when she heard her brother's sleepy voice from the other side of the closed door leading to his bedroom.

'C'mon, Bren. Aren't you done yet?'

'You can come in, if you want.'

The door opened. Sleepy-eyed, tousle-haired, dressed in jeans and a grey T-shirt, Brandon shuffled in.

''Morning, Bren.'

'Good morning, Brandon,' she replied icily, continuing to look at herself in the mirror as she rubbed cream onto her nose.

Brandon splashed water on his face. 'What's the matter with you?' he asked, taking his toothbrush and the toothpaste from the medicine cabinet.

'Matter?' She shot him a look. 'What could possibly be the matter?'

Brandon, brushing furiously, shrugged. 'Don't know,' he said through the soapy froth, blithely indifferent to his sister's black mood.

Brenda set her make-up down very carefully, as if she might hurl it if she didn't maintain a tight self-control. 'Don't know what the matter is, do we? Haven't got the slightest idea?'

She turned on him. 'Well, let's see, shall we, buster? Picture this:

'Your sister – *your* only sister – is dating your best friend.'

'But this best friend has an old girlfriend. Not just *any* old girlfriend – the world is full of those – but one of the most recognizable faces on the whole darn planet, right up there with Julia Roberts.

'Well, but that's okay, because the old girlfriend is about ten-thousand miles away.

'Only one fine day, she shows up at West Beverly, where all the so-called young sophisticates go bonkers, absolutely nuts! And when this "best friend" goes all to pieces himself, what does my dear brother do? . . .

'He goes absolutely ga-ga over the old girlfriend himself! Yes sir, level-headed Brandon leaves not only his dear sister to deal with all this herself, but he spurns his *own* girlfriend for good measure! And then he *flaunts* it at the Peach Pit in a disgusting display!

'It's totally insane, and I would've never believed it of you, Brandon!'

'Bren, it's not like that at all,' Brandon sputtered in protest, a thin white trickle of toothpaste running down his chin. 'I'm shocked you could even think that.'

'Are you? Really?'

'C'mon, you knew about my assignment. I was only with Nicole because of my assignment. Ask Andrea. She wasn't upset. She gave me the assignment herself. She'll tell you.'

'Oh, she's told me plenty. How could you!'

And with that, Brenda Walsh turned her back on her twin brother and marched downstairs.

*

Brenda looked good, and she knew it. That was why she was able to react with such aplomb to the sight of her parents and Dylan cozily drinking coffee around the kitchen table.

'Morning, Mom . . . Morning, Dad.' She kissed each of them on the cheek. 'Hello, Dylan,' Brenda added as if it were a frosty afterthought.

Dylan was clearly uncomfortable. And it didn't help at all that Brenda's parents were hovering about.

'How about some breakfast, dear?' her mother asked. 'I could whip you up some French toast.'

Brenda's nose wrinkled in disgust. 'No thanks, I'm having a difficult time digesting anything French at the moment,' Brenda replied, much to her parents' bafflement.

She fixed Dylan with a direct, challenging gaze. 'Besides, Mom, Dylan's here to take me to breakfast.'

*

Andrea Zuckerman had agonized through a sleepless night, too. She was an intelligent girl, ambitious, strong-willed and proud.

She knew what she wanted and she knew how to get it. She had fallen for Brandon in spite of herself. But when she fell, she fell hard.

But it was alright, she had told herself, because Brandon wasn't like so many of the other boys as West Beverly High. He had what so many of them, born to wealth and certain of their futures, lacked.

Good character.

In Brandon, she saw her male counterpart; someone with strong values, someone who was a leader, who didn't follow fads. Brandon would never have his head turned by someone as trite and shallow as this Nicole Didier. Just because she was famous and beautiful and desirable and . . .

How could she have been so wrong!

Andrea was a regular volunteer at Rap Line, West Beverly's hot line for teens in crisis. And in the pre-dawn hours, she had played a game with herself.

She had listened to so many anonymous girls' voice, anguished over their faithless or cruel or thoughtless boyfriends, that she could easily play both parts. In the darkness, in her mind, she was both the caller and the counsellor:

'Hello, Rap Line. This is Andrea.'

'H-Hello, this is – Well, my name's not important. I–

I'm just an average girl, a student, perhaps someone like you.'

'It's alright, you don't have to give your name. We can just talk. What's the matter?'

'W-well, it's my boyfriend. I guess he's my boyfriend. You see, I've never really let myself think of him that way . . .'

'Yes? Go on.'

'Well, we . . . we were getting along . . . so well. I was really happy, happier than I've ever been . . .'

'Yes? I'm here.'

'I . . . g-guess I let down my guard . . .'

'What do you mean?'

'I fell in love.'

'Hello? Hello? Are you still there?'

'Yes, Andrea. I'm still here . . . It's, it's just that . . . I thought it would last forever . . .'

'I know you're unhappy—'

'I'm miserable, Andrea.'

'But, you'll see, things will get better. You'll find another boyfriend—'

'Not like him.'

'Oh, believe me, there are other fish in the sea.'

'No, no, it's not like that. I don't want another boyfriend. I want him. I want him back. I want it to be like it was.'

'Do you want to tell me what happened?'

'He's fallen for this other girl. I know he has. But it was my fault. I should've never made him spend the day with her. How could I have done it? I don't know what I was thinking. She's this famous French model . . .'

'YOU TOO??'

Andrea woke with a start. In a daze she dressed and set off for school.

Chapter Fifteen

Duke's, on Sunset, was an L.A. tradition, but it wasn't the kind of restaurant that was conducive to a private conversation.

For one thing, there were almost no private tables. There was, instead, a small counter and several long communal tables, with ten or more people crowded together at each one.

For another thing, Duke's attracted a show-business crowd – a mix of actors perusing the trade papers, rock 'n' rollers scarfing down breakfast after an all-night gig, directors and producers cutting deals – and it was a high-decibel kind of place, where everyone had an ear cocked for everyone else's business.

Most of the waiters and waitresses affected the L.A. punk look, with lots of teased, day-glo hair, tattoos and leather; and they, too, were always ready to pull out a glossie or a demo tape at the slightest provocation. In short, it was Dylan's favourite hang-out. He'd once confided to Brenda that he liked it because Tom Waits, his favourite singer, used to practically live there in the days when he was still a struggling blues musician playing in seedy bars around L.A.

Truth be told, Brenda didn't much care for the place, although she'd never told Dylan that.

It had been an uncomfortably silent ride over, but Brenda knew enough not to force the sometimes maddeningly taciturn Dylan to speak before he was ready. Sometimes, she thought, she could almost hear the workings of his mind.

Finally, they eased into the only two empty seats in the noisy, crowded little restaurant. Their hardbacked wooden chairs faced each other at the centre of one of the long tables.

Brenda was more than usually uncomfortable. To her right, was a tall, sallow-skinned would-be rocker, thin as a rail with a huge mane of frizzed-out black hair and a leather jacket open over his bare chest. Opposite him was his girlfriend, a petite, freckle-faced blonde with big green eyes, who was wearing a hot-pink tanktop and appeared to be no more than fourteen.

They were arguing heatedly about the relative merits of some obscure speed-rock band Brenda had never heard of.

On her other side, Brenda was relieved to see, was a very prim-looking little old lady, with old-fashioned rhinestone-trimmed glasses and a straw hat with a red flower in the brim perched jauntily on her wispy white-haired head. Across from her, a brooding, straggly-bearded actor was leafing through Dramalogue, looking for open casting calls.

As they sat, Dylan gave her one of his isn't-this-too-hip-for-words looks, and she smiled thinly back.

'Help you kids?' It was a motherly tone, but when she looked up Brenda saw that the waitress had spiked orange hair.

'I'm really starved,' Dylan exclaimed, proceeding to order bacon and scrambled eggs, blueberry pancakes, orange juice and coffee.

'Hey-hey, you kids been working up an appetite, eh?' the waitress chuckled, taking a pencil from behind her ear and writing up Dylan's order. 'What'll be for you, Miss, the left side of the menu?'

Brenda noticed the disapproving look the little old lady was giving her and she fidgeted. 'Just rye toast and coffee for me,' she said, glancing over at the white-haired lady, who nodded her approval.

'Well, Dylan,' Brenda began, as soon as the waitress was gone. 'Don't you have something to tell me?'

Dylan gave her a peculiar look, as Brenda sat up as straight and as primly as if she was in Sunday church, so that she didn't bump up against either of the people flanking her.

Dylan looked up and down the crowded table. '*Here?*' he asked incredulously. 'But I thought you wanted to have breakfast.'

'*Dylan!* Yes, *here*,' Brenda said, crossly enough that, although she was whispering, she drew the attention of all their neighbours, even momentarily stopping the great speed-metal debate. '*You* picked this place. I'm not going to sit here and make small talk and pretend you haven't been off with your old flame, Nicole Didier!'

'But . . . you said you *wanted* breakfast. I thought we'd talk later.'

Now, all four of the people around them were casting appraising glances at both Dylan and Brenda; they'd all recognized the name, *Nicole Didier*.

'I just said that to get us away from my parents. What's happened to you, Dylan? Did you take a stupid pill or something?'

The green-eyed blonde snickered, then quickly looked down at her plate.

'Whoa, wait a minute.' Dylan held up his hands. 'Lighten up, willya?'

'Why should I?' Brenda shot back.

' 'Cause I'm really wiped out. I've been up most of the night.'

'Is that so?'

'Yeah, that's so. I spent the night with Nicole.'

Brenda froze. The bearded actor looked up, a quizzical expression on his face. The white-haired lady gasped and pursed her lips.

'Well, I never,' she muttered.

The rock 'n' roller gave Dylan one of those man-to-man looks that Brenda just hated. 'Way to go, bro,' he said.

'Shut up, Stevie,' his girlfriend said. 'Mind your own business.'

Brenda couldn't believe it. Just then, the waitress arrived with their food.

'Toast and coffee for you, dear,' she said. 'And here's the right side of the menu for you, stud.' She set the plates down in front of them with brusque professionalism. 'Just holler if you need anything else.'

As the waitress sashayed off, Brenda arched an eyebrow. 'Perhaps I should holler right now.'

'Hey, wait a minute, Bren. Just calm down,' Dylan implored. He took a deep breath. 'Look, that didn't come out exactly right, that bit about spending the night with Nicole.

'I mean, I didn't "spend the night with her", not the way this dude here thinks,' he said, pointing at leather-clad Stevie.

'Hey, man, did you or didn't you?' Stevie asked.

His girlfriend, Susie, rolled her eyes in disbelief, as if

she couldn't believe her boyfriend could be so obtuse. She threw her hands up. 'I don't know what to do with him,' she said to Brenda.

'I've got the same problem,' Brenda replied, and to Dylan she said, 'Well, did you or didn't you?'

Not only Brenda, but all four of the strangers around them were now staring at Dylan, waiting for his answer.

'Wellllll . . . yes and no.'

The little old lady clucked her tongue. 'Young man! Really!'

'I mean, I did spend the night with Nicole. But we just talked. All night. Nothing more. Honest.'

'Talked?' Brenda repeated, as if she were holding the word at arm's length. '*Talked?*'

Stevie snickered. 'Yeah, right,' he said under his breath. 'Likely story.'

'Stevie,' the petite blonde girl snapped. 'Don't press your luck here. Not if you expect me to believe you the next time you come home and tell me you were just out all night rehearsing with the band.'

'But, baby . . .'

Brenda and the white-haired lady both gave the girl approving nods. 'Good for you,' Brenda said. 'We don't have to take lame excuses from the likes of *them*.'

'Hey, girl,' the glam-rocker whined. 'Who asked you?'

Dylan scowled at him. 'Who asked *you*, bud?'

'Don't change the subject,' Brenda cut in. 'You did spend the night with Nicole Didier?'

'*Talking*,' Dylan repeated emphatically.

The actor scratched his beard contemplatively, peering myopically into Dylan's face. '*You* spent the night with Nicole Didier? The model?'

'Buzz off,' Dylan said, ignoring him.

The rock 'n' roller came to the actor's defence. 'Hey, I

don't believe it either, man. A girl like that French model spending the night with *him!* . . . No way.'

'Hey, cut that out!' Susie ordered, pointing at Brenda. 'Can't you see that's insulting to her? Besides, you're no great catch yourself!'

'Girls,' the white-haired lady declared solemnly. 'I'm very proud of how you two are standing up for yourselves. Why in my day, we treated our men like they were little tin gods, and believe me, that didn't do either us or them any good.'

'Thank you, ma'am,' Brenda replied politely, all of a sudden feeling like a little girl in Sunday school being praised by her grandmotherly teacher.

And, like that little girl in Sunday school that she had once been, when the absurdity of their situation struck her, Brenda got the giggles.

Reflexively, she caught Dylan's eye, and saw a look of amusement and affection.

'Can you believe this?' he asked quietly, indicating their four tablemates, who had fallen to squabbling among themselves.

Brenda's shoulders shook with suppressed laughter. She nodded helplessly.

'Let's get out of here,' Dylan said, pushing his chair back and standing.

The old woman wagged a bony finger at Dylan. 'Now you treat this little girl here with respect,' she admonished him. 'And stay away from that French hussy, you hear?'

'Yes, ma'am,' Dylan replied deferentially, pulling out his wallet and throwing two ten-dollars bills down next to his huge platter of untouched food.

As they hurried for the door, the actor called out, 'Hey, lover boy, mind if I finish your breakfast?'

Dylan and Brenda collapsed in helpless guffaws.

CHAPTER SIXTEEN

By the time she stepped off the bus at the West Beverly stop, Andrea had pulled herself together.

There was something soothing, and nurturing, about starting off her day in the back of the bus with all the Hispanic housemaids, who generously helped her practice her Spanish grammar, en route to their well-to-do 'families' in Beverly Hills. Their simplicity, directness and high spirits in the face of adversity never failed to steady her for the rigours of the school day ahead.

The morning air was crisp and fragrant, and its heady scent revived her on the short walk to the school.

Andrea's buoyant mood lasted only a moment, though. Then she saw Brenda and Dylan strolling together across the broad, dewy lawn.

They looked like old times. Not that they were holding hands or kissing or anything like that. But there was something *easy* and relaxed about the two of them that convinced Andrea that they were together, a couple, again. And that, she found profoundly depressing.

Not because she was a mean-spirited girl; on the contrary, although she presented a tough, no-nonsense exterior, underneath Andrea was sentimental, through and through.

And she'd grown to genuinely like Brenda, despite her shallow friends, Kelly and Donna. (She'd even learned, from Brenda, that Donna and Kelly, West Beverly's 'credit card queens' had feelings, too.)

So, she wished her friend Brenda well. It was just that if Brenda and Dylan were back together again, it could mean only one thing:

Brandon had fallen for the French siren's charms.

*

Andrea took her usual seat in Biology class, between Kelly, who was already there, fidgeting, and Brenda, who arrived just as the bell rang. Brenda was, in a word, glowing.

'*Well?*' Kelly hissed in a stage whisper, leaning forward across her desk. 'Did he or didn't he?'

'Settle down, class,' intoned Mr Winchester in a deep voice, his bald dome glinting under the fluorescent lights. He nodded in the direction of the three girls. 'I want your undivided attention.'

Brenda smiled beatifully.

'Today, we're going to discuss sexual reproduction in the animal kingdom. We'll begin with a reading from the *Encyclopedia of the Animal Kingdom*.'

The girls took out their notebooks. Even before Mr Winchester began his lecture, Kelly was scribbling furiously on a scrap of paper with her gold-plated Cross pen.

' "In asexual reproduction there is a splitting of the

chromosomes so that the genetic make-up of . . . the result of this division . . . is the same as that of the parent (unless there is mutation which is always a possibility,)" the biology teacher read in a monotone.

Kelly took the scrap of paper, folded it once and, when Winchester was looking down, threw it on to Andrea's desk.

Andrea glanced at it before she passed it on to Brenda. In childlike block letters Kelly had written, DID HE OR DIDN'T HE?

'Does anyone know what this product of asexual reproduction is called?'

Reflexively, Andrea raised her hand. With her other hand, she surreptitiously threw the paper on Brenda's desk.

Mr Winchester called on her. 'Andrea Zuckerman.'

'It's called a daughter cell,' she said.

'That's correct, Andrea.'

The note came back. Again, Andrea glanced at it before handing it over to Kelly. Below Kelly's question, Brenda had written in her flowing, perfectly formed cursive handwriting, *Yes and no. He spent the night with her in her hotel, but he said nothing happened. They just talked all night.*

' "By combining the nuclear chromosomes and genes from two people," ' Mr Winchester droned on, ' "there is great scope for the production of new genetic patterns, albeit within the make-up of the species." '

Back came the note. DO YOU BELIEVE HIM? Kelly had written.

' "Essentially the process is made up of the union of a male gamete . . . with the female gamete." Does anyone know what these are called?'

There was a flurry of uncomfortable shifting in the classroom. Brenda was busily writing her reply.

'Miss Walsh? How about you?'

Brenda looked up, smiled sweetly. 'Sperm and ovum?'

'Correct, Miss Walsh.' Again the teacher turned away, and again the note dropped on Andrea's desk.

Yes! Brenda had written emphatically. *He said Nicole had changed a lot, that she was a troubled girl despite her fame. He said he felt concern for her. Nothing more. Besides, she's in love with somebody else.*

Andrea's heart sank.

Kelly only took time to underline her previous question before ping-ponging back the note via Andrea's desk.

DO YOU BELIEVE HIM?

' "Theoretically, it would seem to be a simple enough process to bring together two prepared cells from the bodies of the same species," ' the Biology teacher droned on, his voice seeming to recede into the background as Brenda painstakingly wrote out her reply. ' "But in practice with both animal and plant life, the process is often complex. The methods which have been developed to achieve this seemingly easy process are often extremely complicated and, very often, quite strange." '

When the note once more landed on her desk, this is what Andrea saw:

Dylan said if I had doubts, I should ask Brandon. He would know.

'Can someone give us an example of this "strange" process, in hydras, for example?'

Slowly, wearily, Andrea put the note in Kelly's eagerly outstretched hand.

Like any good teacher, Mr Winchester had eyes in the back of his head. 'Miss Taylor,' he said, turning abruptly and glaring at Kelly. 'Perhaps you could enlighten us about the unique reproductive practices of these aquatic animals?'

As quickly she could, Kelly crumpled the note into a tiny ball.

As if deep in thought, Kelly gazed up at the ceiling, resting her chin on the hand holding the balled-up note. 'Hmmm, the hydras,' she said.

Winchester had had enough. 'If you don't know the answer, Miss Taylor, perhaps you could read that note to the entire class?'

Kelly popped the little paper ball into her mouth and swallowed hard. 'What note, Mr Winchester?' she asked innocently.

Chapter Seventeen

Andrea – so sensible, so focused – floated through the rest of the school day like a somnambulist, in a stunned daze.

It was only when she finally got to the newspaper's office and sat down behind her editor's desk that, for the first time since Biology, she felt okay.

For several minutes she just stared down at the page one layout of the next issue. There was a big white space where Brandon's article was supposed to go.

She sighed and checked her watch. He still had twenty minutes to get it in before deadline.

'Hey, Andrea, whadaya say?'

She looked up slowly. Incongruously, Steve Sanders was standing there. What was *he* doing in *her* newspaper office?

'Why, hello Steve. What brings you here?'

Steve unbuttoned his monogrammed blazer and hooked a thumb in his Cardin belt. 'Just came by to say hello, that's all.'

Andrea shrugged. 'Well . . . hello.'

A long, uncomfortable moment passed. What could the boy want? she wondered. Andrea glanced down at her page proofs, then back up:

Steve was still there. He shifted from foot to foot, staring intently down at her through half-lidded eyes. She waited, but he said nothing.

'Steve . . . is there something you want to say?'

He went from one tough-guy/male-model pose to another – tugging his collar, hitching up his slacks – and finally ended up with his hands on his hips. 'Well, you know Andrea, I've been thinking about how you and me don't see very much of each other. Except when we're with the guys, I mean.'

'I thought, maybe, now that you and Brandon aren't an item anymore . . . Well, you know, maybe you and I could, um, go out or something.'

'I see.' Andrea took off her glasses, set them carefully down on her desk and rubbed her eyes. Steve grinned at her.

She *could* see it all clearly: Kelly whispering in her ex-boyfriend's ear . . . Steve desperate for a date – especially one who'd be grateful for his attentions – ever since he and Kelly broke up . . . Kelly and Donna giggling and whispering behind the scenes.

'Steve . . . are you hitting on me?'

'Well, you are kinda cute. And maybe you could, you know, help me with my homework.' The grin widened. 'Whadaya say, Andrea?'

She wanted to punch him one, right in those perfect teeth. Instead, she put her glasses back on, carefully adjusted them on the bridge of her nose and took a deep breath.

'Steve . . . I've been in the office a while, so I'm not quite up on all the latest news.'

'Yes?' He formed a helpful, paternal expression on his bland face.

'Well, there hasn't been a nuclear war or anything, has there?'

'Huh?' His supercilious smile dissolved in confusion. 'Whadaya mean? . . . Of course not.'

'Then you're *not* the last man on earth?'

'I, uh . . .' Steve drew himself up to his full height. 'I, uh . . .'

Andrea gave him her sweetest smile. 'Come back when you are,' she said.

*

Ten minutes later, and Andrea was still staring down at the page one layout. A shadow fell across her desk.

'Hey Andrea, whadaya say?'

Not again! She slammed her blue pencil down on the layout and, eyes flashing, glared up . . .

But it wasn't Steve Sanders. It was Brandon who was standing in front of her desk.

'Whoa!' He backed up a step. 'What's the matter with you?'

'I, uh . . .' Trying to recover, she glanced down at her watch. 'It's deadline. You're late,' she said gruffly, clearing her throat.

Brandon grinned, checking the watch on his own wrist. 'Five minutes to,' he said.

Andrea tried to maintain her composure while looking her boyfriend – her *ex*-boyfriend – in the eyes. She nodded reluctant agreement. 'Five minutes to,' she repeated sadly.

'Hey, you're still not upset about that insanity last night, are you?'

Andrea forced a weak smile. 'No, of course not,' she said.

'Good,' Brandon said briskly, all business.

He dropped several neatly typed pages on the desk. 'Well, here it is. It turned out to be kinda personal, so you might want to run it on the editorial page.'

'Kind of personal?' Andrea repeated wanly.

'Yeah, I hope it's not too much of a drag to change the layout. Listen, I'm running really late; I've gotta get to work. Wanna meet me at the Pit later? You can tell me what you think.'

He seemed so sincere, he was so handsome. 'Sure,' Andrea said helplessly.

Chapter Eighteen

Mulholland Drive was a two-lane blacktop that snaked along the spine of the Santa Monica Mountains, which separated Los Angeles from the suburban bedroom communities of the sprawling San Fernando Valley.

It was a road for lovers and late-night drag racers. At its easternmost tip, high above the Cahuenga Pass and the Hollywood Bowl, was Lookout Point, a turn-off with the kind of panoramic view of L.A., from the spires of downtown all the way to the Pacific Ocean, that otherwise could be seen only from an airplane.

At sunset, Dylan's black Porsche was parked at Lookout Point, and he and Brenda were sitting on the edge of a rock outcropping, their legs dangling off into space. Off to the East, it was night. Below them twinkled the lights and freeways of the vast city, spread out jewel-like, like the nervous system of some fabulous science fiction creature. To the West, the sun's fiery red disc descended into the inky waves.

They spoke in hushed whispers. 'Back in Minnesota, we used to call this river-banking,' Brenda said.

Dylan gave her a quizzical look.

'Parking, necking, you know.' She giggled. 'Instead of Mulholland, we had the Mississippi River. It flows right between Minneapolis and St. Paul.'

Dylan affected a shocked look. 'You mean you necked before you met me?'

A faraway look came into Brenda's eyes. 'There was this boy in tenth grade . . . Bradley Abbot. Well, it was nothing like you and me. It was just puppy love, I suppose. When I told him we were moving to California, he promised one day he'd come after me . . .'

Dylan picked up a pebble and threw it into the void. 'And when he does, I'm sure *I'll* handle it much better than you coped with Nicole,' he declared, sounding totally unconvincing.

'Hah! Yeah, right . . . Tell me, what was it like?' Brenda asked softly. 'You and Nicole . . . before.'

Dylan shrugged. 'Like you and Bradley, I suppose.' He thought a moment, trying to put that faraway time into words. 'We were kids,' he said at last. 'We were in love. It was wrong. It's history now.'

The darkness deepened. The dying sun sent streamers of light dancing across the distant waves. 'Go on,' Brenda said, squeezing his hand. 'I want to know.'

'She was kinda like you back then,' Dylan recalled. 'Bright, pretty, energy for miles . . . and new in town.'

Brenda nodded; it was strange, but she felt a surge of sympathy for her famous French rival.

'She was just this gangly kid from Paris. She spoke English as a second language, didn't know a soul at West Beverly – you know how hard that can be.'

'Sure,' Brenda agreed. 'We had cliques and stuck-up girls back in Minneapolis, but nothing compared to here.'

'On top of all that, she lived this secluded life at the embassy – sort of like being in a monastery.'

'Convent,' Brenda corrected.

'Yeah, whatever. The point is, she was alone a lot of the time, even at school; and when she wasn't alone, she was hanging around adults – I mean, *staid* adults; you know, the foreign-policy striped pants set – being her father's hostess at all these boring teas and cocktail parties and receptions and things. You know, making small talk with some white-haired old fogie, that kind of thing.

'She was desperate to talk to somebody her own age. You could see it in her eyes. I could anyway, even that first time at the French Embassy. That's where we met.

'My old man dragged me to one of these boring "functions" I was telling you about. I didn't know why at the time; it's not like we ever had one of those father–son relationships where your dad takes you to the ballgame, you know?'

'I know,' Brenda said with quiet empathy. She'd seen Dylan and his father up close – too close – and well knew how thoughtless and what a petty tyrant he was to his son. And she herself was blessed to have the kind of father who'd taken Brandon and her to Twins games ever since they were old enough to pick up a bat and glove.

'Well, I should've known. "Black" Jack's mind is always working,' Dylan's lip curled derisively around his father's nickname. 'And what it's always working on is another angle. One of his companies had some business to do with the French government, and he knew that the Ambassador had this daughter who was my age. Well, ol' Jack figured it might do him some good if his kid and the Ambassador's daughter . . . Well, you get the idea. Only I guess he never figured it would turn serious, *real* serious.'

Brenda couldn't suppress a momentary, almost instinctive flicker of concern from her face.

'But the thing is, it wasn't like you and me,' Dylan quickly assured her. 'I mean, I'm not trying to tell you we weren't crazy about each other or anything like that. But it was like you and this Bradley guy. It was . . . puppy love.'

Brenda considered Dylan's trip that had so scandalized the West Beverly student-body sophisticates. 'Did you fly to Paris on account of "puppy love"?' she asked.

'Sure,' Dylan replied without hesitation. 'Just like this Bradley swore someday he'd fly to L.A. for you.'

Brenda traced a check mark in the air with her index finger. 'Score one for you.'

Dylan's dark, brooding eyes focused somewhere in the middle distance. But he wasn't looking at the lights of the cars streaming up and down the Hollywood freeway and their delicate firefly traceries; it was the past he was seeing. 'I'm not trying to tell you that was all it was. What threw us together, after those first days, was what wanted to tear us apart.'

It took a moment for Brenda to figure out what he was talking about. 'Your dad?'

'And hers. The more they insisted we stop seeing each other, the more nuts for each other we got. It just seemed so . . . so . . .'

'Unfair?' Brenda suggested.

'Yeah, that's how it was. *Unfair*. You know how kids are. We had a passion alright, but it wasn't just for each other, it was for justice, too.'

'But all those rumours—'

'Oh yeah, well, Nicole and I gave the gossips a lot of material to work with. No question about that.'

The pride evident in his voice made Brenda smile. The way varsity athletes showed off in their letter sweaters, the way Steve Sanders treasured his Corvette, Dylan took pride in his outlaw reputation.

'Oh I'm certain of it, too,' Brenda agreed dryly. 'But there's one, uh, bit of particular material you gave the gossips that we haven't talked about yet.'

She let the unspoken question hang in the cool night air.

'The baby,' she said at last.

'Yeah, the baby. That was the thing that burned the circuits in my brain.' A gust of wind carrying the scent of the distant ocean mussed his hair. He seemed to grope for the right words. 'All that boring stuff they made us study in Human Development class – you know, the responsibilities you have when you bring a new life into the world.' Dylan looked down. 'When you think it's really happened, all of a sudden all those trite sayings are like some incredible weight.'

His mouth worked silently. 'Now I know if you and I ever . . .' The words drifted off on the rising wind.

Strands of Brenda's auburn locks whipped across her narrowed eyes. 'Dylan! Can't you see what this is doing to me?' she pleaded. 'I mean it's great that you're so damn responsible.' Dylan looked up at her. '*Really*, I mean it. It's not something I'd expect from a lot of other guys . . .' She sighed deeply, trying to calm her turbulent emotions. 'I *am* trying to understand.' She gazed into his eyes. '*Are* you the father of Nicole Didier's baby?'

She hoped for a simple no, but feared an equally simple yes. The answer, though, turned out to be more complicated than that.

'She wanted people to think I was.'

'*What?*'

'Yeah, at first it sounded kinda crazy to me, too. You gotta remember that last night was the first time we'd talked, *really* talked, since Paris, and that was a long time ago. Until last night, the rumours and the gossip were all that *I* knew, too, just like everybody else.

'Last night was the first time I learned the truth. Maybe last night was the first time Nicole even admitted the truth to herself.'

And so, finally, as Brenda listened raptly and a crescent moon rose in the sky, Dylan explained:

The Ambassador, Nicole's father, had hated Dylan, and not just because he was his darling daughter's first love. Like Jim Walsh, the Ambassador despised 'Black' Jack McKay, and he had extended his antipathy towards the son. Only, unlike Brenda's father, the Ambassador had never got to know Dylan on his own terms, and so had never got beyond that first intense dislike.

Naturally, when 'Black' Jack's French business schemes had come unravelled, he, in turn, blamed the fiasco on his son. And so he, too, tried to keep Nicole and Dylan apart. It was the only thing 'Black' Jack and the Ambassador ever agreed on.

Then had come the argument at the French Open, followed by the scene at Orly Airport, when *gendarmes* were called in to forcibly put Dylan on the plane back to L.A. A few short weeks later, Nicole – a complete unknown – was on the cover of European *Vogue*. The interlocking, insular worlds of high fashion and high society were dazzled by the Ambassador's fresh-faced daughter. From afar, Hollywood took notice. Nicole's meteoric rise had begun.

Months passed. In Europe, Nicole seemed to be everywhere, on the cover of everything. Then, still in the first year of her success, she went from the fashion pages and the society columns to her first brush with the Fleet Street tabloids and the gossip columns.

The teen beauty with the madonna glow had had a baby!

At first, the press and the public were scandalized. But she seemed so innocent, so unspoiled, despite the screaming headlines. And in one of those rare quirks of timing, of public temper, of fate . . . the press and the public were charmed.

So the innocent beauty was a devilish girl, too, but she endured the media's crass attentions with such grace. Her celebrity only grew.

But one man was most definitely *not* charmed. The Ambassador. And he demanded an explanation *immédiatement*.

Nicole adored her new life – the glamour, the adulation, the fame. But her distinguished father was in a rage, he threatened to banish her to a convent, and her new life was on the line.

The solution turned out to be simple. She told him the American boy, the impetuous one, who was thousands of miles away in Beverly Hills, California, was the one. And she promised her father the Ambassador that she would never see Dylan again.

'Then *who?*' Brenda whispered urgently, as if coming out of a trance. 'Whose baby was it?'

Dylan, the keeper of a secret, smiled enigmatically. 'You saw him the other day. The whole school did.'

Brenda was aghast. 'Not that old fat guy in the rumpled seersucker suit?'

Dylan laughed. 'No way.'

'Then *who?*'

'The photographer.'

'Who?' Brenda's brow furrowed in puzzlement. '*What* photographer?'

'This older guy, thirtysomething, goes everywhere with her. She said he's doing a book about her.

'His name's Roland something. I actually remember him from Paris. I only saw him for a minute. He came up to us at this outdoor café, introduced himself and gave her his card. We laughed about it. "A professional fashion photographer, oh sure." But he's the guy who first made her famous.'

To distract herself in the days following Dylan's expulsion, Nicole had taken the photographer up on his offer. Roland's instinct and his professional eye were justified as soon as he saw the contact sheets from that first photo session. Nicole was a lovely girl in person, but through the camera she was one in a million, with an ineffable quality that couldn't be taught or created by artifice. She had *it*.

And like Pygmalian in the Greek myths, Roland fell for his model, and she was in love with him. But Nicole was still a minor, despite the sophisticated adult world she began to live in, and she was still subject to her father's will.

To blame Dylan for the result of their union seemed so logical to Nicole then, and it meant that Roland could travel with her and the child without arousing suspicion. She would tell her father the truth when she came of age.

But then the whirlwind of her career – successful beyond either of their wildest imaginings – took over their lives. And in the past year, an insidious evil had darkened Nicole's days.

'Nicole told me she has a drug habit,' Dylan said. 'It's something she only faced for the first time yesterday.'

'Yesterday?' Brenda had been ready to whoop for joy at the outcome of Dylan's tale . . . until he came to the last line. Her voice filled with alarm. 'But she spent yesterday with my brother!'

Dylan stood, held out his hand and raised her to him. 'Don't worry, Bren.' He put his arms around her waist. Behind them twinkled the fairyland lights of the city. 'You've got to start trusting the men in your life,' he grinned. 'Especially me.

'As for your brother, his head wasn't turned by Nicole any more than mine was. In fact, you could say it was the other way around. She said it was Brandon who convinced her to tell everything – and I mean *everything* – to her father.

'She and Roland flew to New York this morning. Tomorrow, they're taking Concorde to Paris. The Ambassador's going to find her a discreet clinic in the countryside and she's promised to check herself in.'

Chapter Nineteen

It was almost closing time at the Peach Pit when Andrea finally arrived.

She'd supervised the school paper's press run, as she did every week, and she carried with her an early copy, as if it were a talisman against her suspicions and fears, to show Brandon. The article he'd written (which, at his suggestion, she'd run on the editorial page) was so good, so sensible and to the point, that it had allayed the worst of her fears. But she still had questions . . . and suspicions.

Brandon was wiping off the counter when she entered. Scott and David, the two feckless freshmen, were the only customers left in the little place.

'Hey, Andrea.' Brandon greeted her with a warm, carefree smile.

She rummaged in her shoulder bag and pulled out the early copy of the newspaper. 'I thought you'd want to get a first look at your handiwork,' she said non-committally, dropping the paper down in front of him.

'Well,' Brandon asked playfully, wiping his hands on his apron. 'Does Mademoiselle Editor approve?'

When had he ever called her *Mademoiselle* before? 'Except for the fact that you turned in an editorial which I could've written in the first place myself, I guess *Mademoiselle* does approve. You said what needed to be said.'

Brandon grinned.

'It ran as you wrote it. I didn't change a single word.'

Brandon didn't register the coolness in her voice; he was too pleased and impressed by the lack of real criticism. 'I worked really hard on it,' he said.

'We still have things to talk about, though.'

'Things?' Brandon's eyebrows shot up. 'I thought the piece was okay the way it was.'

Behind her glasses, Andrea's eyes gleamed. 'Not-for-publication things,' she said.

'Aw c'mon, Andrea, you're not still upset about last night. That was nothing.'

'*Nothing?*' Flashing through Andrea's mind were the images of him and Nicole at the première, him and Nicole getting out of the limo, the kiss . . .

The Pit's front door banged open and Dylan strode in. The two freshmen immediately scattered for the exit. Dylan ignored them. 'Hey, Andrea. Yo, Brandon.'

Brandon eyed him carefully. 'Hey, Dylan. How're you doin'?'

Dylan went to the unspoken heart of the question. 'Brenda and I are doing just fine,' he said with a broad, happy grin.

'That's good,' Brandon said solemnly. 'Real good.' Brandon understood and smiled, happy that his sister and his best friend were back together again.

Dylan reached into his pocket. 'I've got a little something for you,' he said. 'A present. From Nicole.'

Andrea was aghast. In Dylan's hand was an exquisite jewelled case. 'Her pillbox,' Dylan said. 'She said to tell you, it's empty and it's going to stay that way. She said to say, thanks for saving her life *twice* in one day.'

Andrea's agitated confusion lasted only a few minutes more. On the drive to her house, Brandon recounted all his experiences with Nicole, telling her especially about the amphetamines that had once been kept in the jewelled case. 'I think you should have it,' he said, when they were parked in front of her home. He pressed the pillbox into her hand.

And in the end, there was only one point that Andrea found terribly hard to believe. 'She practically invited you to spend the night with her!'

'Not "practically",' Brandon said. 'She *did* ask me to spend the night with her.'

'But you refused. You refused Nicole Didier?'

'Mm-hm,' Brandon replied, in a maddeningly taciturn way.

'But . . . but.' For once, Andrea was at a loss for words. 'She's beautiful, she's intelligent, she's famous . . . I don't understand.'

'It's very simple,' Brandon replied as if it were the most obvious thing in the world. He put his arm around her and pulled her close. 'I just told her I already have a girlfriend who is beautiful . . . and intelligent . . . and someday will be famous. And she saw the look in my eyes, and she understood.'

CHAPTER TWENTY

The world of the twin Walshes was seemingly set aright, but there was one matter left that Brandon needed to attend to.

Again, he reminded himself that he was only thirty seconds older than his twin; still, Brandon was feeling the weight of being an older brother again, and he couldn't rest easily until he was certain that things were right with Brenda. He knocked softly on her bedroom door.

Out in the hall, Cindy Walsh was passing unseen with an armload of freshly laundered clothes to drop off in Brandon's room. She wasn't the kind of mother who eavesdropped, but she was concerned about her kids, and she couldn't resist 'pausing' a moment to overhear.

'Come in,' Brenda said to her brother, her voice muffled through the closed door.

Brandon stuck his head inside. 'Hi, Bren.'

'Hi.' She closed the thick textbook on her lap. She was sitting on her bed, wearing her white socks and oversized man's shirt. She gave him a friendly, relaxed smile. 'Everything okay with you and Andrea?'

'Yup.' Brandon stepped into the room. 'I hear you and Dylan are okay, too.'

Her big smile was all the confirmation he needed.

'Then I guess there's only one more thing.'

'What's that Brandon?'

'You and me. I just hate it when we argue.'

'Oh.' Brenda shrugged dismissively. 'We'll always be okay.'

'It didn't seem like that yesterday.'

Brenda felt more than just lucky – how many other girls had a brother this concerned? 'Hey, we're siblings,' she said lightly. 'We're supposed to argue, but we'll always make up.'

'That's good,' Brandon said with feeling. He glanced all around the room before his eyes finally fixed on the newspaper in his own hand. He looked at it as if seeing it for the first time. Holding it out to her, he added quietly, 'I just wanted to make sure.'

Brenda took it from him. She saw his byline under the title, *STAR-TRACKING AT WEST BEVERLY HIGH*.

'Read it,' Brandon urged her. 'Read it out loud.'

Brenda smiled warmly at her brother; he was like all writers, she was beginning to realize, in love with the sound of his own words. She cleared her throat, smoothed the newspaper down on her lap and read:

STAR-TRACKING AT WEST BEVERLY HIGH
BY BRANDON WALSH

There's a special feeling that we students share at West Beverly High. We feel that we're the best and brightest, the heirs to a proud tradition.

Academically, West Beverly is one of the top three schools in the entire country; the newspaper you hold in your hand is ranked first in the nation; our graduates go on to the finest Ivy League universities. West Beverly alumni run Fortune Five Hundred corporations, they head leading scientific institutions, they hold high posts in government.

But this past week, we've all seen that proud tradition debased.

And you and I and the faculty and administration are all to blame.

When was the last time the school scheduled a special assembly to honour a medical researcher or a physician or a political activist who had once graduated from this school and had gone on to make a difference to the community?

The answer is . . . Never.

Make no mistake, Nicole Didier is a fine young woman with a high-visibility job that makes tremendous daily demands on her. I've seen her race through a typical day, and it's not only physically draining, but emotionally and spiritually as well.

But while her job – and it is a job – may be glamourous and risqué enough to set tongues wagging, her job is not brain surgery, nor does it make a real contribution to the community.

And until we honour our true heroes, who do make true contributions and a real difference to the world, we won't be living up to the tradition that should be the very essence of West Beverly High.

And until that day, you and I will be nothing more than star-struck star-trackers. And there is nothing that is more uncool than that.

Brenda looked. 'Wow, Brandon. I'm proud of you. *That* is going to hit a lot of people right in the ego, right where they live.'

Outside, Cindy Walsh, a proud and relieved expression on her weary face, tiptoed away.

Back in Brenda's room, Brandon brushed a fall of hair out of his eyes. He gave his sister an aw-shucks look. 'I just thought it needed saying, that's all.'

His sister gave him a mischievous glance. 'I suppose this means I'm going to have to throw all my Parisian Girl perfumes away.'

Brandon did a double-take.

The Walsh house rang with peals of laughter.